When Witches Sing

ADVENTURES IN LEVENA: YULETIDE SPECIAL

AELINA ISAACS

NESHAMA PUBLISHING

Contents

Dedication

To those who aren't who they used to be, and wouldn't have it any other way.

Before Reading

This book takes place after Phantom and Rook, specifically during the eleven year span before the epilogue. I have kept the details of this era vague, but everything mentioned will be further explored in the main novels of the series. This novella is intended to be a wholesome, quick read. With that being said, the characters were greatly affected during that decade and some consequences are inevitable.

Warnings include descriptions of a disassociation episode, discrimination, graphic sex, smoking, and swearing.

Happy Holidays,
Aelina

What's In A Word

The 'Old Common' used in the book is based on the Hebrew language, and some meanings have been adjusted to fit the story. They are listed here in the order they appear.

Mashallah: Let it be done
Nesiga Mayhim: Water Extraction spell
Kul Sheresh: Root Formation spell
Hahlama: Healing
Abracadabra: Life
Tchotchke: Small Thing
Meira: Light
Lechem: Bread
Leva: Heart

The Years Between

Glitter and Glue

Felix
Five Months After Thatch Left

I've officially decided that glitter is the *worst* thing to ever be invented.

Witch House is empty, a rare thing these days. I managed to convince Dad–*Arlo*, that I'm not feeling well, not that I would need much of an excuse to stay home from school. He knows I like going, so if I want to stay home, there's a good reason.

But I'm not sick.

Oh, my nerves are shot and my glued together fingers shake. But that's only because I didn't sleep last night, and pounded a half a pot of coffee the moment everyone left for work or school this morning. An hour later and the excess caffeine hasn't relented, but whatever.

This *has* to be perfect.

I stand on wobbling legs, the sensation in my toes long gone from sitting cross-legged for nearly an hour. I hold the banner up, inspecting my work. Mountains of purple and silver glitter cascade down my front. I frown at the drooping letters. A few of the pasted on, gigantic paper letters flop to the floor with simultaneous wet slaps, leaving behind a partial message.

'HA PY B RTHD Y A LO'

"Shit," I mutter, blowing out a heavy breath.

"Don't let Arlo hear you talking like that." A distorted voice softly chides, scaring the fucking *shit* out of me.

The banner goes flying overhead and I *squeak*. Magick flares and rattles the paintings on the walls. I inhale sharply and contain my energy before causing a disaster. *Again.*

Silas tucks his chin into his left shoulder, but instead of the usual loud *hum* that follows the movement, he laughs. In the few months we've been living together at Witch House, I've never heard the sound. It's ... probably frightening to anyone that doesn't know him, but I like it, screechy rasping and all.

"You're supposed to be at school." I mumble, hurrying for the banner now cast across the craft table behind me. Before I can crumple it into a ball, Silas' hand falls on mine.

"Don't do that," he says, and I frown.

"It's not good enough."

Silas shakes his head. Thick white bangs sweep back and forth across the bridge of his nose, hiding his eyes from me. Another thing Silas doesn't let the world see. His hair is longer now than when we first met. The near pearlescent tresses sweep beyond his shoulders when he takes the banner from me. I reluctantly let him have it with a huff.

Silas studies the mess of a banner that I had intended to hang in the kitchen downstairs before Arlo and the others got home, but at this rate it'll never happen. He gently lays it down on the craft table, allowing rivers of glue and glitter to flow onto the table's paint streaked surface. The metal accessorizing his pitch black, wrist to ankle ensemble jingles as he moves. All bracelets and chains, harnesses and necklaces.

He asks, "It's Arlo's birthday?"

I nod, rocking back and forth on my sock covered heels.

Silas' fingers twitch. "He didn't say anything."

I roll my eyes. "Yeah, well, that's D—Arlo, for you. He didn't ..." I gesture vaguely, searching for words that won't betray Arlo. "He didn't get to celebrate last year, for his centennial. It's ... kind of a big deal I guess, turning a *hundred*."

To my surprise, Silas snorts. "So old."

I blink rapidly. "Did you just ... joke?"

Silas lifts his head and gives me a look, or at least I think he is. His lips push together like they usually do when he's not impressed, and he crosses his arms. "I can be funny."

"*Right,*" I say, unsure what to do now.

"Can I help?" Silas asks, gesturing to the banner. "We can make a new one. You were using too much glue. And glitter. Less is more with these things."

"Oh," I say dumbly, not expecting that. It's not that we don't get along, we just kind of ... *exist* next to each other. I'm always being weird and breaking shit, he's always on the outside looking in, aloof but not in an unkind way.

Silas turns away with something reminiscent of a soft chuckle, but to others it could be considered an evil villain laugh. "If we take this downstairs, I can bake and give you directions on how to properly make a birthday banner. Two birds with one stone, as they say."

Without warning, heat swarms my cheeks and neck upon remembering the cake Silas made for *me* in the fall. It was really good.

I nod. "Yeah, okay. If you're sure you want to help, I'd like that."

It starts with a slow, upward tugging of one corner of his pale lips, but a wide smile ends up transforming Silas' features. "I want to help."

Twenty minutes and five trips up and down the stairs later, we've set up shop in the kitchen. I was afraid of making a mess in here, and frankly after last week's debacle with the stove, I try to stay out of the kitchen as much as possible. Silas assures me that it'll be fine, so I leave it to him to clean up any wreckage I leave in my wake, which he agrees to with another smile.

Weird.

While the oven preheats, Silas helps me roll out another length of six inch wide paper on the floor, this sheet a bright pink. We make it long enough to fit the wide archway separating the kitchen from the dining room. Silas suggests we write the message in glue and spread glitter over it, instead of cutting out and individually pasting each letter to the banner.

Why didn't I think of that?

"Will it have enough time to dry?" I ask, and Silas nods.

"It should. I'll start on the cake, if you've got this."

I wave him off. "Yeah. Good idea, by the way."

Silas opens his mouth, closes it, then starts again when he gestures to the banner. "Shouldn't it say Dad or something like that?"

Heat flushes my neck and I shift uncomfortably. "Oh, I don't—it's, you know ..." I chance a look at Silas who hasn't moved a muscle, waiting patiently for me to continue. "It's early, isn't it? Shouldn't I wait?" As the words tumble out in a rush, a weight falls from my shoulders. I've been wrestling the word *Dad* farther down my throat ever since Arlo adopted me, not wanting to seem too—

"Says who?" Silas counters, and I scoff.

"I *dunno.*" I snap, crossing my arms like he does. "Aren't people supposed to be—"

Silas puts up a hand, showing off painted black nails. "I'm going to stop you right there. Anything involving the words 'supposed to' is generally not true. Do you see him as your Dad?"

I reluctantly nod, grumbling. "But won't he feel uncomfortable? What if he doesn't see me as ... as his son?" I admit, near quiet and breakable.

"Felix, you *are* his son." Silas whispers, incredibly soft and strained. He extends his hand to me, then thinks better of it. "Don't worry about it, okay?"

"Yeah, okay." I shrug, unfolding my arms.

Silas dips his head but says nothing, retreating to the inner kitchen where counters and appliances reign. I sigh and settle on the floor, facing the banner. I carefully write the message in a large, flowing script that I've been told multiple times is exceptional, but I think looks messy.

I take my time like Silas said, laying down one letter at a time in glue, gently spreading glitter over it before going on to the next. I have to blow my hair out of my eyes a few times. I've decided to try growing it out, and I'm not sure how I feel about it yet. While mine doesn't grow as fast as Silas' does, it's long enough to be in the way.

We work in companionable silence and I glance over at him a few times, only able to see the top of his head from my place on the floor, and with the counter island separating us. He appears to be in his own little world, though. Hair bouncing softly as he enjoys the music that must be blaring in his earbuds now.

I *do* want to know more about him, and maybe become friends, but I have no idea what to say to him. On the bad days when I can't separate other people's thoughts from my own, I've stolen glimpses of Silas' mind.

It's *loud*.

That's why I don't feel so bad for not pursuing conversation, and allowing him to take the lead. Or so I tell myself, which sounds better than sounding like the clueless kid everyone sees me as. While I'm not an adult, I'm *not* a kid anymore either. It's easier to talk now than it used to be, but not always. I had thought I would've grown out of it, but ... here we are. Words are still my enemy, but I have more tools to fight them.

I decide to be a little brave. If Silas didn't feel like interacting, he wouldn't have offered to help, right?

"When's, uh, when's *your* birthday?" I ask, head ducked as I work.

He doesn't say anything.

I peek up and find him standing in front of the oven with his back to me. I don't ask again and he doesn't move, so I go back to work. A few minutes pass in silence, then the gentle thud of Silas' boots cross the room towards me.

I swallow heavily, pretending that I don't notice.

He sits cross-legged across from me, hands tightly gripping his knees. I warily look up through my hair, shaking it out of the way so I can see him better. His back is ramrod straight, head tilted as he watches me. One side of his lips twitches into an almost smile.

"What?"

"You should let me pin your hair back, you've got glitter and glue all in it."

I balk, reaching up to inspect the hair in my eyes, realizing a moment too late that's a bad idea. I groan, setting down the glue. I glare at Silas and he chews on his bottom lip to keep from smiling again. I itch to throw him off, just a little.

"Fine, only if I get to do yours," I say without a second thought, then am immediately horrified. I'm good at braiding hair, Kleo made me do hers all the time, but Silas doesn't seem like the kind of person who enjoys being touched. "Nevermind, I didn't–"

Silas hums in a short, loud burst, and the sound of it reminds me of an aborted laugh. I imagine if I could see his eyes, they'd be widening. He lifts his left shoulder and rubs his cheek on the peak of it, then regards me once more. I never flinch from his movements or noises, and the others don't either. At least not on purpose.

Silas' outbursts can be sudden and there's been a few times when he's been especially startled. His magick lashes out like my own, breaking things, but it's always an accident and it embarrasses him. So I don't flinch.

I shrug, picking the glue back up. "I'm just joking. You can ... you can fix it, if you want, my hair. It's kind of in the way, I don't know how you do it all the time. But you don't have to, though."

Silas scoots back, allowing space between him and the banner. He crooks a finger in a 'come hither' gesture. I oblige, leaving the glue behind. My cheeks flush and I sit before him, unsure what to do.

"I don't have any pins," I say.

Silas reaches into his pants pocket, revealing a handful of bobby pins.

I nod once, giving him a sideways smile. "That's handy."

"Do you mind if I listen to music while I do this?" Silas asks, drawing his hand back.

I shake my head, drawing my knees up to my chest. "No, you don't gotta ask. Thanks for letting me know."

Silas nods, tapping the side of the earbud buried in his hair. His mouth twitches and he doesn't move, so I close my eyes.

A moment passes.

Then, ever so gently, cold fingers brush against my temples. I fight the shiver threatening my spine as he twirls a patch of hair, then pins the twist back against my crown. He repeats the process, my hair not quite long enough to be fashioned in any neat sort of way. I've never had *my* hair done before.

I breathe.

And he breathes.

I tilt my head, catching the subtle sounds of Silas' music. I strain to hear it better, and it must be wicked loud if *I* can hear the interwoven harmonies of a violin and an electronic beat. Silas doesn't resume his work so I clear my throat and open my eyes.

He's *grinning*. "I can see you."

"You're one to talk." I roll my eyes, huffing out a laugh. I gesture to his hair. "Ready?"

Silas tenses, then nods. I don't ask again, because I have to believe that he'll tell me if he's uncomfortable. He reaches into another pocket, then offers me a hair tie. I've never seen him use either accessory, I wonder why he carries them around.

Before I can say anything, he turns around and puts his back to me. I drop my knees and spread my legs out on either side of his curled body. "Okay," he says, sounding anything but.

I roll my bottom lip between my teeth. Chocolate fills the kitchen and I fill my lungs with the warm scent, then exhale a question. "Would you mind if we ... listened together?"

Silas sharply glances back at me over his shoulder, throwing white hair from his eyes. For the briefest of seconds, I catch a glimpse of icy blue.

"You won't like it."

"How do you know?"

He shrugs, turning his attention ahead once again. I take that as an answer and gently touch his shoulder as a warning before moving to his hair.

"Tilt your head up," I ask softly.

Silas doesn't move, at least, not in that way. He reaches into one of his cargo pockets, taking out a phone. After a few seconds of messing around on it, music begins to spill from the phone's speakers instead of the earbuds. Sure enough, an energetic violin is accompanied by a modern and electric beat, forming a refreshing melody. He sets the phone down outside of my legs framing him, then tilts his face to the ceiling.

"Thanks," I say, then gather three incredibly soft chunks of white at the base of his right temple. Silas shudders and I pause. "You alright?"

"Yes," Silas says immediately, then hums long and low before answering again, a pleased sound. "I've never had my hair done before. It feels nice."

I laugh quietly. "Me either, until now. Trust me, I know what I'm doing. Kleo *loves* her hair being done."

I wait another moment, then start braiding the chaos witch's hair.

It takes longer than it should have, and not because of how long and *thick* his hair is, but because we both can't stop moving to Silas' music.

It started with Silas. He would bob his head or his fingers would dance on his thigh, then stop, as if catching himself. After the third time he cut himself off, I softly began tapping my toes on the floor and swaying back and forth, gentle as to not pull his hair. I added humming for good measure, but otherwise kept the silence between us.

With each noise and small movement that I made, Silas' shoulders lowered and loosened until he was happily moving in place and humming along with me. Then, he started to tell me *about* each song that came on, all composed by the same violinist.

And I listened.

Now, I secure the tail of the main braid. A masterpiece, if I do say so myself. Numerous plaits begin at the front of Silas' pale head. A main one lays in the center and three on either side which interweave with each other, snaking back and forth until meeting again at the base of his neck. The end of the singular, thick braid running down his spine comes to an end between his shoulder blades. I gently lay the white against his black shirt.

"Finished," I announce softly, not wanting to move. I haven't paid any attention to Silas' face, not even when I uncovered it bit by bit, braiding his bangs back into the center section. I wanted to wait until all his hair was restrained, but now a swell of nervousness rushes over me.

I take a deep breath upon realizing the feeling is not mine.

He's nervous.

"How does it look?" Silas asks quietly, staring straight ahead.

"Well, not to brag, *but* I think it's pretty epic, like the old warriors from legend."

Silas snorts, then abruptly stands. "I better go check the cake."

"Oh, right," I say, watching him walk away. I sit there, feeling empty and a little disappointed, but unsure why. I decide not to dwell on it and just be thankful that he trusted me to be in his space, and that he shared his music which is deeply personal to him. I spin in place on the floor, checking out the banner that was once behind me.

I smile at how beautiful it turned out, poking the glue to ensure it's dried.

I stand with the banner in my hands and turn, coming face to face with Silas who snuck up on me and is so incredibly close. And there he is, I can *see* him.

Oh.

"What do you guys think you're doing?"

I startle out of my skin and throw my hands up. Before the banner can go flying, Silas is there, hands blanketing mine. Both of us look at the smiling man leaning in the open doorway leading from the kitchen to the backyard.

An *incredibly* long silence follows.

I scrape my brain for something, *anything* to say, but of course, Silas saves me.

He gently releases my hands, then waves to Arlo with eyes so bright my heart does a weird little flip that *hurts*. Silas says, "Happy Birthday, Arlo. You're supposed to be at work."

Arlo raises a brow, and the smirk upon his face widens. "Thank you, Silas, but you're supposed to be at school." His eyes slide from Silas to me, and I can only awkwardly wave. "And you're *sick*."

"Hey, Dad," I say, lofting the formerly unspoken name into the air like a bomb. I inhale sharply and my heart pounds in my ears. It's soon overwhelmed by the sparkle in Arlo's eyes and the soft laugh that bubbles from his chest. I smile then, and add, "Happy Birthday."

A Little Bit Longer

Silas

One Year Since Thatch Left

I stand at the threshold between pebbles and forest, unsure whether to invade the Hedge Witch's private moment. A violin married to a comforting beat produces a calm presence that rests only in my ear drums. I hum along to the tune, fingers twitching with indecision. I'm sure he knows I'm here. I'm the definition of *not* subtle. I know this.

I tap the side of one ear bud, silencing the music.

Laughter and music echoes through the woods behind me, a distant reminder of the day's celebrations that are taking place without us. It's the first Game since Thatch disappeared, or rather the day it would've been if the Game still existed.

No one has mentioned it, or Thatch, and thus far have smoothly referred to the festival taking place on the mainland by its new name. *The Min Festival.*

A festival that Arlo won't allow us to attend, for reasons beyond me. He's become increasingly paranoid, not wanting anyone to leave the island without a companion, travel stone, and cellphone. I had thought that he, Elochian and Quentin solved the Leon problem, but perhaps I was wrong. The AWO and NOJ have been quiet ever since, but that doesn't mean they're gone.

I close my eyes and breathe, envisioning what waits at home.

Witch House has red and orange banners decorating the windows and porch. Candles burn in every window, all reds and oranges and yellows. Gourds and pumpkins have claimed the backyard, those of the painted and carved variety. We grew them ourselves, well, it was Felix mostly. He has a tendency to bring life to anything he touches.

Buffet tables full of crockpots and random tupperware dishes wait in the backyard too, with a big bonfire that perfumes the woods, accompanied by our trusted family and friends. In a few hours, when dusk hits, we'll tell stories around the fire. Stories of my family's life, and the history of where we live, who crafted the earth and have watched over the people living upon it.

Family.

After a year, that word still stumbles in my mind, trips up my tongue. I don't think of Arlo like a father. There was a short time I was fascinated by him in a different sense, and that prevented any father-son feelings from forming. Not that I ever told him, that would be embarrassing. Now, he's my best friend. Someone I would live and die for, and he has done the same for me.

I open my eyes.

Arlo hasn't moved from his vigil with the old stone by the river.

I take a step forward. My shoes crunch through dead leaves, twigs, then fall upon pebbles and squish into stinking washed up seagrass. Before coming to Arlo's side, I press my forehead to the pillar composed of bedrock and fossilized life. An ancient energy courses through my cold veins, electric and intense and *overwhelming*.

I gasp softly, my eyes burn.

But another energy, one that is younger and warmer, all safe and love and *homehomehome* intertwines with it. I swear that the whisper of *'please come* **home***,'* escapes through the cracks in the stone. Perhaps the words were poured into the pillar in hopes of reaching someone across space and time, but the universe is rejecting the plea.

I don't comment on it.

Instead I place my palms upon the cool, craggy stone on either side of my head. Without the fringe that interrupted my vision for years, the icy blue glow surrounding my hands is plain to see. Oh it's still long, down to the middle of my back now. Felix loves it, and I love it when he braids it. Most of the time, I allow him to. It's an excuse for us to touch, because the thought of asking him to touch me all of the time is frightening.

And exhilarating.

I exhale, relieved to leave behind some of the frantic energy trapped inside my soul. Parties, or rather any gathering with lots of people, especially kids, is a guarantee for chaos to ensue. I ensure to soften the magick pouring into the stone with an intent of *'hello we are here, we are waiting for you.'*

I breathe deeply, leaving the stone where it has stood for thousands upon thousands of years. I turn to Arlo, who has not moved other than to turn his head towards me. He gives me a soft smile, and his magick touched emerald eyes are glistening. His hair is loose and wild, twisting in the wind. I can't help but notice how cold he looks, but I don't say anything.

I stand by his side, and we watch the river in silence. This is how we most often spend our time when it's just us, standing by this river. I don't mind.

A loon calls from a small island across the lake. Otters disturb the water to the east of us, flipping and playing, chittering at each other without a care in the world. Felix reminds me of an otter, and I've told him so. Even if I *could* forget things, I would never be able to forget how red his face got and how much he smiled despite the fact he didn't want to.

I smile, just a little bit.

A small tree limb unwillingly follows the soft current wrapping around our island, drifting to the east, to the otters. The smaller of the two finds it, and it's not long before they're both submerging the branch until its green and wilted leaves flutter under the water, only to let it *pop* above the surface.

Out of the corner of my eye, I notice Arlo watching the empty sky. There's a few storm clouds in the distance where the ravine lies, but otherwise it's the perfect day for an outside celebration. Sunny, but chilly enough to need a few layers. The breeze is something that caresses you instead of assaulting. It's when a flock of black necked geese and a protective pair of shepherding wyverns fly overhead that I'm able to hazard a guess as to what he's thinking. He's always thinking, about so many things.

Felix accidentally read his mind once, and he cried for hours afterwards. That was the first time I held him in the dark. He had come to my room in the night after stumbling upon Arlo sitting alone in the kitchen, staring off into nothing. He kept saying, *'He smiled at me, and he looked* fine, *Silas. How could he have* smiled *at me when he was hurting so* much.*'

"Do witches have more than one familiar?" I ask, keeping my gaze trained on the birds.

Arlo chuckles softly, but there's no humor to it. "Hm, I'm not sure. I don't know any witches who outlived theirs, but then again, Bosko and I found each other much later in life than most do. He lived a good life, and the old man deserves his peace."

I nod, tapping my thighs rapidly. Bosko passed in his sleep on the last day of October, a few days ago. While Arlo says it was old age, there's something that itches my brain, insisting that he's lying. But why would he lie?

"Are you okay?" I ask in a strangled rush that scrapes my throat. My voice will be a constant reminder of my first family. Iris and Arlo have taught me sign in the last year, which I prefer, usually.

Arlo smiles but doesn't look at me, lifting a shoulder. He's wearing his threadbare rainbow duster that really needs to be tossed or patched, holding it tight around himself as he stares over the water like the widows do in the movies. "I'm fine. Just thought I'd wait here awhile. In case, you know?" He laughs then, shaking his head. "Pretty silly, isn't it?"

"No," I say, using more force than intended. I soften my tone, or at least, the best I can. "I'll wait with you."

And I do.

We stand together for a long time, then settle for sitting cross-legged on the grassy banks where Thatch's den once lay hidden. It's still there, but devoid of its contents. I'm pretty sure Arlo and Felix spent the day down there last week, but neither have brought it up. I swing my feet over the shoreline's edge, trying to think of what to say.

"He's coming back," Arlo says, interrupting my train of thought with three barely spoken words that are infused with a contrasting, firm confidence.

I nod. "I know."

"You should go back to the party, they'll be missing you." Arlo gestures over his shoulder. "I'm surprised Felix hasn't showed up yet."

I don't tell him that Felix is the one that sent me after him. "And you. They'll be missing you, too."

Arlo smiles again. "I'm just going to wait a little bit longer."

When I make it back to the cottage, Felix accosts me immediately. He doesn't come right into my personal space or say anything, but he practically vibrates with excitement whilst awaiting an update. His eyes glitter between pink and gold, but he doesn't appear to be affecting anyone or tossing objects by accident. He's gotten alot better at managing and controlling his magick, but emotions can get the best of anyone. I know that.

I dip my chin and hum in consideration, then say, "He's waiting."

Felix lets out a breath, swiping a hand through his hair which hangs around his ears now. I like it this way, and I've told him so. He made sure to tell me that he wasn't copying me, but I made sure to tell him it was alright if he was. He's wearing his leather jacket with his name stitched on the front, a sibling to the one Arlo made for himself shortly after Thatch left, and it doesn't quite fit Felix at all anymore. He shot up this past summer, legs and arms no longer gangly but long and lean. Everything about him became *more* this year, in ways that I'm having trouble with.

Finnegan stands beside Felix, holding his elbows and unusually quiet. He and Arlo both have been weird, and it's affecting everybody else. The bizarrely similar pair do everything together, from saving the island to cooking dinner. His cool gaze sweeps across the party, over the numerous witches younger and older than me, over the original Misfits who are watching us with intent. There's so many people that live here, add the Mainlanders and it's instantly a party. The latest eye patch that Arlo crafted for him seems to fit much better, and he's squinting less. Finnegan catches me studying him, a teasing brow raises and the corner of his lips quirk. His leather jacket creaks as he reaches up to push away the long brunet curls that have cast over his nose. Every interaction with the reporter feels like a test, and even worse, I want to pass every one. It's no secret that without him, we wouldn't have stood a chance on our own.

Out of everyone to ask, Felix's gaze turns back to me. "What do we do?"

My lips push together and I hum, pulling the sensation from deep within my chest, fingers twitching. I study the decorated and well lit cottage. The pumpkins, hanging lanterns, tables of food, red and orange and *home*. I give the witches my attention briefly, then look back to Felix.

I say, "We wait with him."

Twenty minutes later I find Arlo in the same spot, overlooking the river and bruised sky. His deep thoughts must be obscuring my arrival, his brow is furrowed and jaw set tight. I clear my throat before the raucous group approaching the beach startles him.

He jumps to standing anyway, eyes wide as he takes me, and the rest of us, in.

"Silas, what ..." Arlo starts, then is reduced to a loss as magick permeates the air, thickening the warm fall evening with ozone and *rightness*.

Tobias, Felix, and the other witches orchestrate tables, decorations and gourds through the air. Candles dance in the atmosphere above the celebration unfolding on the beach, waiting for a place to land. Kitt and Lindsey set to work on organizing the area, whilst Quentin and Loch are in charge of corralling the children. Doc hauls a massive pumpkin that has yet to be carved on one shoulder, holding their wife's hand with a free paw. Gowan and Iris crouch before the stone pillar, arranging something.

Caspian wheels over to us, a wreath of flowers bounce in his lap as his chair's wide tires climb the rugged earth. Finnegan accompanies him, one of Arlo's beanies in hand. Arlo stares down at his Caspian, mouth open and hands shaking. "What's this?" Arlo finally asks quietly, eyes unable to stop darting between the gathering and us.

"We wait together," I say, promptly ducking my chin into my shoulder. I rub, the fabric against my cheek distracts me from the unpleasant feeling crawling throughout my nerves.

Caspian nods, offering Arlo the flowers and a knowing smile. "Silas' idea. We should've thought of it sooner. From now on, we'll have our fall festivities down here. Just in case."

Arlo's cheeks flush and he takes the wreath with trembling fingers, sparking green eyes. For the briefest of moments, he locks eyes with Finnegan, then his gaze skitters down to the wreath in his hands. He releases a shuddering breath, caressing the petal of a freshly picked sunflower. Caspian and I exchange a look while Arlo stares at the wreath with reverence.

Eventually, he lifts his head and smiles at all three of us. "He's coming back."

"I know."

And we wait together.

Come On In

Calen
Six Years After Thatch Left

When I unlock the front doors five minutes early, there is a line of people waiting to enter the only store left standing in the North End of Levena. Mr. Lincoln stands at the forefront with a smile and a coffee in each hand. I hold the door open with my boot, taking the warm beverage he offers.

Before he can ask, I say, "Oatmeal and toast."

He nods with a knowing smile, dipping his thick peppered beard onto his snowflake dotted chest. I take a sip, sighing when the perfection from the little cafe several blocks to the south hits my tongue. Together we greet the dozen or so regulars who have nothing better to do during the week then visit Primo's.

None of them *live* in the North End, no one that has money does.

Snow falls in lazy spirals, small flakes that are nothing compared to the storm we had last night. I came up an hour early so I could shovel out the storefront, big piles lay on either side of the wide sidewalk that leads to the main street. The others didn't like the idea of me spending any more time than I have to up here, but duty calls.

Mr. Lincoln is a big man in every sense of the word. Despite his age, he has this effect of instantly making you feel like he'll protect you from anything. Deep lines crease the human's eyes and mouth, all won through a good and happy life. He's the one who got me this job in the first place, and I'll never forget his kindness.

He's also the only person who knows my secret.

"How're your fingers today?" He asks, nodding to my fingertips.

Nearly every digit is covered in bandaids, and I flex them a little, chuckling. "Oh fine, I think I might try playing again today."

We step inside and wipe our snow touched boots on an old entry rug that lays over a patterned electric blue and white carpet, shutting the doors behind us. "Don't push yourself birdie, that violin isn't going anywhere."

The name tag pinned to my denim overalls doesn't proclaim Birdie, or my real name, but something generic. Alex. I readjust my gray woolen beret, fighting the urge to roll my eyes at the old man. "A couple of minutes playing around won't hurt. I just *need* to figure out this melody."

Mr. Lincoln walks me to the cashier's counter that is centered in the back of the store, wandering through aisles upon neatly organized aisles of vinyl records. On the outskirts of the store are record players for sale, ranging from the cheaper tabletop variety to more expensive consoles handcrafted from the finest wood. I've sold none of the stock in over a year.

"Still on about that?" Mr. Lincoln asks, tapping the counter's surface to a tune that must be in his head. He stands on the customer side of the counter while I keep the register company. I sigh, hooking my thumbs around the straps of my overalls.

"I'm telling you, I *heard* it somewhere, it's not mine. I'm not taking credit for someone else's song. If I can remember the rest of it, then maybe I can search for it better." I shrug, voice turning almost shy, "in the meantime, it's fun to play."

Mr. Lincoln smiles, and we shoot the shit for a little while longer. The regulars we had welcomed into the store have already found their usual places. Four sit in the reading area where couches, books on music theory and entertainment magazines reign. Three sit together at the coffee bar, a small nook beside the reading area. A few more patrons peruse through records they swear they'll buy next time, and the three kids who practice before school are already setting up in the band area.

The band area is my favorite part of Primo's.

In the corner a drum set, keyboard, cello, bass, and old school piano are always set up, while more instruments are nestled into racks on the two walls cradling the holy place. Guitars, saxophones, clarinets, lutes, mandolins and so *much*. But there, on the right wall beside a large photograph taken of Primo during his first concert, are the violins. Only two, but they are everything.

The college kids start to play.

Goosebumps creep across my arms, up my neck. I shudder when the first person strokes the ivories with reverence. Another grins wide, strumming upon their guitar with a gentle rhythm. The third takes a deep breath, then exhales into their saxophone. Snow falls lazily outside the windows, heavier now but beautiful all the same.

Algae bulb chandeliers reflect warm light throughout the store decorated like a vintage hard rocker had sex with a modern classist and this is the love child between them. All bright, wide and open, accessorized with framed newspaper articles and photographs of those who once frequented this store but went on to bigger and better things. Instruments that were broken in shows and more that are pristine but ancient, hang from the ceiling. Some litter the free spaces between the photos and articles.

My shoulders relax.

Mr. Lincoln takes my hand.

I firmly take his and squeeze.

He squeezes back.

"Do what makes you happy, birdie, just take care of yourself," he says, then joins the regulars who look through records and make a promise to buy something next time, but never do. Like the kindred spirits around him, he never comes here to buy anything.

They come here for the peace found after spending a few moments in this place, at Primo's. Same as I do. Same as Primo once did.

Until he was Stolen.

The day passes in a blur of money and music.

It's been busier than usual and my head rings obnoxiously. I blame the upcoming Yule, evident by the amount of parents shopping for their kids who are in school for the day, adding a card to their bags from the bulletin board which houses information about tutors of different varieties. Most of the tutors are students from the university, but not all.

Mr. Lincoln left after his usual hour that he spends here in the morning. I didn't get a chance to play the melody for him, but the store is nearly empty now. After eating a late lunch which evens out my shaking hands, I take full advantage and clear a space in the band area. I have to stand on my tip-toes to take my preferred instrument off the wall, but the moment I do it's like I can breathe again.

It's much older than its modern counterpart on the wall, but well kept. The bow takes rosin like a dream and withstands my unique way of playing. The scroll is finely carved and the body holds endless layers of rosewood grain, a testament to the wood's age before it was even crafted into a violin. I perch the instrument in the crook of my neck and rest my chin on the flexible metal chin rest.

A sense of euphoria washes over me preemptively, followed by the distinctive feeling that I'm being watched. My arm pauses in the air, elbow bent and bow held a breath width above the violin. I look around casually, but there isn't anyone on this side of the store. I exhale, refocusing on the instrument. I bring horsehair to strings made of catgut.

'The best strings in the business,' Primo whispers, setting my elbow at the proper angle. I shake it off, he only lives in the confines of my memories now. I'm sure of it.

I play.

I don't work a violin like most people do. In fact, I don't do *anything* like most people do. It wasn't until after *they* made me leave that I stopped pretending to be normal, and by Gods, it's the best thing I've ever done.

I dance.

And I play.

The notes that have haunted me endlessly flow from my brain, down the tendons and muscles in my neck, through my arms. The melody causes my fingers to twitch in ways that I still don't comprehend, like my only home is buried in the notes of the vague song that won't ever leave my mind. I sweep my bow across the strings with a hot need and my nerves stand on end, electrified and wanting. I move side to side, knees bending and hips swaying. I spin in a circle on the crescendo, right foot tucked high onto my left thigh.

I play.

I dance.

And the next notes in the song come to me, *finally*, but they don't escape from my instrument.

My attention jerks to the keyboard where someone plays with a furious and sharp skill I've not heard before, but they pay me no mind. I can't stop playing, can't break this moment despite the fact that this —this *person*— is echoing what's in my mind, and I don't recognize them. To be fair, a black hoodie covers their torso and the hood is pulled up over their face, or what would be their face but a mess of long white hair obscures it. Chains and leather harnesses accessories the black cargo pants they're wearing, and their black combat boots are similar to mine.

I continue to dance.

And *we* play.

The sound we create is not classical by any means. It carries a fast rhythm, accompanied by an electrical beat set by the person's keyboard which partners with his playing and my own. I don't think about the notes or anything else. Horsehairs splinter and shred as I increase the tempo, and my companion's head jerks downwards into their rising shoulder. They don't stop playing, in fact they match my speed and then some. A sudden, deep and almost pleased hum emanates from the person and vibrates my chest, lighting me on fire from the inside out.

I decide immediately that I want to know this person. No, *need* to know this person.

We finish, and silence overtakes the world.

My feet firmly plant on the carpet after a last spin. My fingers ache and they're warm, some are slick with the evidence of cuts reopening. Chest heaving and sweat dripping down my brow, I turn to officially introduce myself to my companion, to demand how they knew that *song*.

But they're gone, leaving behind no trace that they were ever here to begin with.

When Mr. Lincoln greets me the next day with an extra cup of coffee and a smile, I can't bring myself to play out the script. I blurt out, "There was someone here yesterday afternoon, Mr. Lincoln. I was practicing and then they appeared out of *nowhere*, playing right along and then some, because they knew the song, Mr. Lincoln. We *finished* it, you should've heard us, it was *everything*."

The old man's face goes through several transformations while I hurriedly relay every detail, save for the bleeding fingers which have been freshly rewrapped. Excitement, confusion, interest, and then, a softening of his wrinkles. He asks, "White hair you say?"

My heart leaps and I nod quickly. "Yes, yeah, *yes*."

He doesn't say anything then, instead he leads me inside. We kick snow off our boots just inside the door, then make our way to the cashier's counter. He stands on his side and I stand on the other. He leans down, elbows on the counter, and I mimic him until we're inches apart. Mr. Lincoln looks around the store, but there's no one here out of the ordinary, and they're busy with their usual things. Music starts in the band area from the college kids, but it's dull compared to what happened yesterday.

Mr. Lincoln whispers, "He's like you, birdie."

My breath catches. Brain grinds in the confines of my skull. Heart stammers. Mr. Lincoln smells like coffee and snow in the sun, which grounds me. I say, "I thought there weren't any left in Levena."

He shakes his head. "They're not in Levena. Waiting until the time is right."

I swallow something heavy, almost afraid to ask. My fingers tremble and my vision pulses, stomach churning coffee and nothing else. "How do you know this?"

Mr. Lincoln smiles, but says nothing on the matter. Instead he says, "He's a shy fellow, but if you ask for help, he'll offer it, hide you somewhere safer than here. Please, tell me you'll ask, birdie."

I blink, unsure what to say. I can't tell him the truth, not all of it. He knows I'm not working for myself, that the money I make goes to someone else, but what he *doesn't* know is it's not *one* someone. It's multiple hungry mouths, most of which are too small to go hungry, and the rest are those who protect them.

I could never leave them.

Mr. Lincoln must see it in my eyes, because he takes my hand and squeezes it with a sad smile. "Think about it."

I say the only thing I can think of. "I don't think he'll be back."

Mr. Lincoln reaches into his jacket pocket, withdrawing a small white paper bag. He offers it to me without commenting on my obvious lack of breakfast, and I take the bag with a fruit laden pastry tucked inside. I thank him and start eating, staring off into nothing as my thoughts trip over themselves.

His smile brightens from something melancholy to hopeful. "He will."

He doesn't return.

Night has fallen and the store is closed. I lock the doors. Vacuum the floors. Wipe down the counters. Straighten the reading and band areas. Pull the curtains shut. I stand in the back of the store, overlooking my work. With a singular nod of satisfaction, I turn off the lights. I'm not afraid of the dark, and that's exactly what the main floor is now, drenched in pitch black.

But I'm a demon, and it's in my nature to see through the dark. After going through the back hall, I find the innocent looking door sitting across from the public bathroom and a weight leaves my shoulders when I open it. Another day without getting caught.

I enter a storage room filled with boxes of holiday decorations, new records that I have to put out tomorrow, and so much junk that I'm quite sure not even Primo would know what's in all the totes and boxes. If he were here, that is. If the clutter doesn't do it, the dust and overall *old* smell that thickens the air is enough to drive away any prying eyes.

I shut the door behind me and block it off using waist high speakers that blew last month, ones that used to fill the store with music of Primo's choice, usually old rock. In all reality, the people hunting us down can get through the pathetic barricade easily enough, but the sound will give us time to escape. I sigh at the thought, reminded of what Mr. Lincoln said.

But how could a young witch who is *also* hiding, help someone like me?

Like us.

In the back right corner of the narrow room is a pile of cardboard boxes. Sharp black marker denotes one as 'kitchen.' Another is 'Primo's stuff,' while the last simply says, 'articles.'

With the same care that I give these boxes every night, I move them out of the way. One by one, I gingerly pick up the awkward and slightly falling apart boxes and set them in a horizontal line against the back wall. A wooden trapdoor with an iron ring and scuffed grain is revealed, and I knock on it twice.

Pause.

Three times.

Pause.

Once.

A series of clunks and clicks occur, then the door swings down into seemingly nothingness. I stand at the precipice and cross my arms over my chest, hands tightly gripping the opposite shoulder, then jump.

As I fall, three things happen, as they do every night I go home.

Magick dissipates, leaving me temporarily cold until the illusion completely leaves. An illusion that Serena casts every morning, further disguising me. Great leather wings tipped with ferocious talons unfurl and catch air as it rushes by, slowing my descent. Small horns curl beneath my beret, lifting the hat a smidgen. A velvety orange tail with a heart-shaped black point snaps back and forth, cracking through the air.

Voices, such *loud* voices, assault my ears in the best of ways.

And the darkness gives way to the light.

Strings of neon lights line both cornices of the hallway that I land in, boots softly touching cement. Blue illuminates the crooks between wall and ceiling, continuing in a straight line until a large, distant room interrupts the hall. Waiting for me at the end of the hall, their figures shrouded by distance but familiar to me all the same, is my family.

Ramsis meets me halfway, barreling into my chest. The pixie is barely larger than my hand and his glitter freckles shine under the light, further leading someone to believe Ramsis is cute and harmless. In fact, Ramsis is the fiercest person I know, and their shadow magick is terrifying.

Jo is seconds later, burrowing her face into my lean chest. I stagger back a step, chuckling as I wrap my arms around her. Ramsis climbs out of the way to my shoulder, using my overall strap as a handhold. Jo's bright red curls tickle my chin, she's going through a growth spurt and will be taller than me I think. She's only ten and has a lot more growing to do, if I have anything to say about it.

Jo tilts her face up, glaring at me. "You're *late*," She hisses, then violet magick flares in her eyes, the only indication I have before she disappears. Oh she's *there*, her body warm in my arms still, but she can bend light in marvelous ways all without trying. In fact, it's when she *tries* that she can't get her magick to cooperate.

"By ten minutes, Jo. The snow is coming down out there hard, and I wanted to do some shoveling so the morning doesn't suck so bad," I say, walking towards our family with Jo's hand in mine.

Ramsis huffs, gently tugging on a lock of my hair that's returned to its natural color, vibrant peach instead of jet black. "And you're *supposed* to let us know if there's a change of plans."

Miles is next to berate me. The oldest of our group, older than me even, stands at the forefront of the welcoming committee with his thick, pale green arms crossed. "I was ready to go up there and find you." He frowns, lips pulling down around his tusks. One is jagged and broken, a goodbye present from his parents, and the other is sharp and long. Initially, Miles was assigned to guard duty because of his size and fierce appearance, but thankfully we've never actually needed him to fight. I learned after he'd been here a few weeks he's actually a complete sweetheart and has *never* gotten into a fight before.

Hopefully that will never change.

Thankfully, Serena saves me from the onslaught of worry. The faun joins my side with a wide grin, arm hooking through mine. Her bright red mohawk shines purple under the blue lights that crawl along the length of the tunnel. "Come on guys, cut Boss a break. We have the emergency system for a reason, and if they needed help, then Boss would've notified us," Serena elbows me harshly, "*right*, Boss?"

"Right," I manage, coughing for dramatic effect. "What's for dinner?" I ask, trying to change course.

Lily laughs, causing snow to fall around her slight body. She presses a dark hand to her stomach, truly amused. "Beans, what else?"

And I can't help but laugh too. Because what else *would* a gang of young witches in hiding eat? What else can I afford other than cans upon cans of beans, vegetables, gross preserved meat, and fruit drenched in a sickly sweet syrup that doesn't belong with fruit?

As I allow my family to lead me to the dining room which is just a corner out of the huge cement dungeon we live in, I can't help but wonder what the white haired man eats. Does he eat out of cans too?

Or is he doing better than we are?

Is he alone? Does he have a gang too?

How does *he* go undetected?

Instinctively, I touch the bracelet on my left wrist, one given to me by the Nightingale herself. A gift I will have to repay one day, and with my life I'm sure. A simple, thin silver band that hides my magick signature and any magick placed upon me, allowing me to hide in plain sight. But like all things, it comes with a cost. It doesn't just hide my signature, it snuffs out my magick completely, leaving me Normal, the only thing Levena allows. The bracelet only comes off once, and when it does, I can never put it back on.

So I continue to do the best I can for those I love, powerless and weak.

Because I do love these people, every single one. I could never leave them.

They have dinner ready at the long table, and no one has eaten yet. We wait, for some are scurrying out of their ironic homes to join us. Homes of steel bars with locks that long ago lost their keys, because this prison was here before Levena was even a thought.

And a prison it remains, because we aren't truly free. Yes, I can go upstairs, and *yes*, I leave this place once a week to fetch groceries, but I'm not free. None of the others covet my position. None of the others want to willingly put themselves in the public eye. This has been my job, ever since I found the imprint of an invisible Jo thrown into a snowbank, a year after the same had happened to me.

Then I found David, sweet David. A shapeshifter who changes form every time he gets excited or emotional at all, and never the same form twice because it happens so *often*. An easy target for the AWO and NOJ.

Next was Ramsis.

Serena.

Lily.

Miles.

Jamie.

And so *many* more. Despite the fact it's killing me slowly, I will never say no to a young witch in need of refuge. I will never forget how it felt to be kicked out, wandering the snow covered streets, on my birthday and *starving* because of something I could not control. How lonely it was, and how I almost died. Not from exposure, not at first.

I was chased, tracked. *Hunted.*

Until Primo offered me his hand and said, "Come with me."

So I did.

I startle awake with no air in my lungs, and the lights have been turned out.

Jo sleeps soundly on the thin mattress we share, unaware that I'm suffocating beside her. I reach for my throat, finding cords and tendons straining for dear life. The moment I begin to panic, all hell breaks loose.

An alarm I never wanted to hear blares, rattling my ear drums, dimming the edges of my vision. A scream bellows over it, echoing through the black, and I think Miles. Oh Gods no, *Miles.* More screams follow and I suck in air, throwing myself out of bed. Magick restrained for years now bubbles to the surface for the first time, demanding to be let out so it can fight, *protect.*

They've finally found us.

Jo wakes, eyes wide and knees knocking together when she springs to my side. She looks up to me and in the smallest voice asks, "Cae?"

I kneel, taking her hands in my mine. I look her straight in the eye. By *Gods* she's a child, but she's not anymore, is she?

"I'm going to clear the way. You remember what to do."

She nods, eyes hardening and jaw setting. "Take the others. Run. Run. *Run.*"

I kiss her cheeks, then her forehead. "Good girl. I love you, JoJo."

"I love you, Cae." Jo sniffs, disappearing and reappearing in my hands. We've been working on extending her invisibility to others, which admittedly would be life saving right now, but we're out of time.

I stand. I face the door to our cell and the hell that lays beyond, because my people are *screaming*. Less than a minute has passed and how many have I lost already?

I breathe, chest heaving with effort.

This is it.

I bring the silver band to my lips and whisper a single word. "*Mashallah*."

It's like trying on an old denim coat with an insulated inner layer, one that was forgotten in the back of your closet but fits the same regardless, and you're so glad to have found it because the bare winter is *cold*. So cold, and you'll be dying in a few months, but this *jacket* makes it bearable, providing a shred of warmth, of something *familiar*.

And *I* scream.

A shock wave of sound reverberates through the prison, skipping over those my magick deems friend, family, *good*. My lungs empty with such a force that a giddiness overwhelms me, a feeling that says *yes*, and this is who you *are*, and thank you for letting me be *free*.

Light bulbs shatter.

Bones crack.

Concrete fractures.

Our world shakes.

But it's not enough.

I take three steps into the darkness and am immediately assaulted by enemies immune to my power. Solid pain throttles my jaw, rocking my head to the side. A gloved hand encapsulates my mouth. A knife flashes and this is it, isn't it?

Something warm spills across my throat, but it doesn't hurt. I belatedly think that it should, but all I can think is Jo. Ramsis. Miles. Serena. Lily. David. All of them, I've failed them. There's no way they could've escaped in time.

The hand falls from my mouth.

The solid *thud, thud, thud* of bodies falling rattles my nerves.

A singular orb of white light appears before me, cradled by a man with numerous white braids pulled back into a ponytail. His face is visible now, and my breath hitches, because Gods, his *face*. The orb of light shoots upwards, expanding until it's a mini sun that illuminates the chaos that's invaded my home. Black clouds float at waist height throughout the space, encasing enemy bodies. I'm reminded of mini thunderstorms, electricity crackles around the bodies inside the balls of chaos. So many came, ready to kill children.

He asks, "Are you alright?"

I'm surprised by the sound of his voice, a hoarse thing that seems like it would be painful to use, but it holds a certain symphony as well. Something *more*. His eyes are full of magick, an icy blue that is near blinding to stare into directly. It hits me then, he's alone. *He's* the one controlling the clouds. There is no one standing behind him, no one else in the prison besides my stunned family and over two dozen assassins restrained by this singular man.

"Who are you?"

He smiles, and it's like his voice, an action that seems like it would be painful due to the hypertrophic scars covering the right half of his face and part of his neck. There's such a beauty to the expression, and I have the sense that it's rare for him to smile, almost like I've discovered a secret. His right eyebrow and eyelashes have been stolen, their counterparts are a beautiful delicate white that matches his hair. I cannot tell if he was burned by fire or acid, but either way he *survived*.

"A friend." He extends a hand clad in a black leather glove, just like the rest of his ensemble. "We don't have much time, it's not safe here anymore. Come with me, I can protect you, all of you."

And Gods, doesn't *that* sound nice? To hang the burden on someone else's shoulders, even for just a little while. But I don't know this man. *Yes*, he just saved my life, and the lives of my family, but to leave everything behind and follow a stranger?

They're looking at me now, those standing around the injured like a barrier. Waiting for me to make a decision, the *right* one.

Do I even have a choice?

"How did you know?"

He blushes, although the right side of his face is already a persistent red and pink that contrasts his pale complexion immensely. "Charles."

Mr. Lincoln, always looking out for me. I suppose if he trusts this man, then it'll have to be enough for me. But how did he know? Did he hear the break in, or see them?

"Boss, we should do what he says. Miles is hurt, bad." Serena calls from the forefront of those gathered. "We're all in agreement over here."

I nod, then take the man's hand. I shake it firmly, receiving a buzzing sensation that travels up my arm, but it's not painful. On the contrary it's peaceful, warm, and focusing. I look him dead in the eyes even though his irises are so intense that my heart skips a beat. "I'm putting the lives of me and my own in your hands. I'm entrusting you to keep us safe, stranger."

With conviction, he says, "I will."

Jo runs over the moment my hand drops from his, leaping into my arms with a barely choked back sob of relief. I hold her tight to my chest, and her legs wrap around my waist. I glance at the clouds of bodies, then back to the man. "What are you going to do with them?"

"Let the laundry hang to dry." He withdraws a black tarot card from his pocket, one I'm achingly familiar with. The line work is gold, depicting a skull with a nightingale perched atop it. He hands it to me and I don't waste time, tapping the bird three times.

The outline of the skull glows a vibrant red, signaling that the Nightingale has been called. Soon her team will come and discover what has happened to Primo's. Oh *no*, what is upstairs like?

My head jerks up and I stare at the distant ceiling. He must see it on my face because the man shakes his head, reaching back into his pocket. "There's nothing for you up there. I have a transportation stone that's big enough for all of us."

I find my voice, but it's small. "The violin?"

"I'm sorry." He shakes his head again, staring at the polished amethyst cut into the shape of an oval resting in his hand. Transportation stones were forbidden years ago, how he has such a large one I have no idea. One of many questions to add to the list.

"Oh." I take in a shuddering breath, squeezing Jo closer to my chest. It's just a material thing, this shouldn't affect me like it does. But it does, doesn't it? *Gods*, it hurts. I nod, trying to regain my composure. I look to my family, they trust me to do right by them.

I hope this is it.

With tears in my eyes and a waver to my voice, I beckon them over. "Come on, it's alright. We're going somewhere safe."

They move as a group. David and Serena hold one end of Mile's makeshift stretcher, while Lily and Jamie hold the other end. Silas glances at them, then to me. "We have a healer. He'll be okay. You'll all be okay."

A hand falls on my right shoulder. Another on my left, followed by Ramsis perching on the arch of my left wing. One by one, my family connects in some way, shape or form, and the man smiles a little watching us. Jo lifts her head from the crook of my neck to stare up into my face, and I give her a watery smile. The man extends his free hand to me, the other clutches the stone which glows a soft purple.

I take it, fingers entwining with his like we've known each other forever. A shuddering breath leaves me without permission as I look around the prison one last time. It's been our home for so long, and now ...

A bubble of translucent green magick forms around our party, warm and soft and peaceful. Quiet and unlike anything I've experienced before. He squeezes my hand and says, "Silas."

I squeeze back, unable to stop the upward hopeful quirk of my lips. "Calen."

He surprises me with a sudden and loud hum, like he did when we were playing music together. It strikes me then with such ferocity that the same person who nervously played the keyboard yesterday single-handedly took down a band of assassins, saved us. What is his specialty, I wonder?

A dull roar surrounds us and Jo squeaks, covering her ears. Tension rolls through the group, causing the hands and bodies against me to stiffen.

Then it's over.

We touch down on dirt. *Actual* dirt.

My knees give out. I hold Jo close to my chest, breathing and breathing and *breathing* because there's *trees*.

There's trees with bare limbs and trees with branches laden with needles.

There's birds calling, a soft breeze, and frozen mud beneath my knees.

Smoke lazily rolls from a chimney attached to the most beautiful house I've ever seen. A house with purple shutters and gray paint, a wrap around porch and pretty windows. There's another place behind it, a cottage really, that's just as quaint and beautiful as the main house. A long path is shoveled through the snow to the front door of the house, but footprints and pawprints of every sort litter the yard on either side of the main path.

I'm not quite sure what I was expecting, but a couple of beautiful houses in the woods was not it. Sure the main house is big, but if there's already people living there, is there enough room for all of us?

Silas' humming starts up again, but this time he seems agitated, not pleased. The noises are in shorter bursts and his hands twitch at his sides, sometimes they jerk upwards towards his face as he turns in a slow circle. "What's wrong?" I ask, gently setting Jo down on the snow before standing upright. Her little cold hand settles into mine.

"Nothing, it'll be fine. He won't mind. It'll be fine," he says quickly, and my heart drops.

"What do you—"

The front doors to the house swing open and two men step out, then halt on the porch upon seeing us. One man is much taller and older than the other, he wears a scowl and a black knitted duster that I admire. The other appears to be my age, his hair is long like Silas' but a shining bronze instead of white. He doesn't appear angry like his companion, just very confused.

Silas glances at the men, then back to me. He steps closer and offers me his hand again. "Trust me," He whispers, and I take it without thinking. That startles me, but not enough to let go. I look to my companions and they nod, unsure but determined. They always have my back.

Silas leads Jo and I down the path, followed by the group carrying the stretcher, then everyone else. The two men meet us at the bottom steps of the porch with arms crossed and unreadable expressions that are eerily similar. The older man stares down at Silas, a dark eyebrow arched in question.

"Care to explain?" He asks, voice gruff and perhaps groggy, like he had just awoken. It's then I realize that it's barely dawn, the sky is painted in pastel purples and pinks.

Silas raises his chin, determined. "They need a home."

The younger man only has eyes for Silas, and they soften immensely when he says those four words. His chest heaves with apparent pride, but he doesn't say anything.

The older man sighs, pinching the bridge of his nose. I open my mouth to say something, *anything* to change his mind and convince him to let us stay, but I'm too late.

The man lifts his head and focuses on me, a quiet smile blooming across his face. "Well, come on in then, we'll get you all fixed up."

Not A Skunk

Lysander
Nine Years Since Thatch Left

Mud croaks beneath my toes and the yellow sprouts along my arms grow a few inches, fully content. I jump onto a fallen log slick with marsh and time, putting my arms out to balance myself. When I get to the end of the natural bridge carrying me over a particularly wet spot, I leap off into swamp grass.

I land on both feet, disturbing milkweeds and the monarchs who dominate their pink blossoms. The layers of necklaces adorning my bare chest bounce and tangle together. Bones, coins and other trinkets rattle against each other, music to my ears. My highwaters bunch up just above my ankles, collecting thistles and muck. I slip my fingers into my front pockets, whistling Hook's favorite tune as I continue my rounds.

While I can't see the beast, I can *feel* them skulking in the murky depths encroaching on the small floating islands. The precarious chunks of peat, mud and hidden underwater plants provide the only protection and semblance of solid land in this marsh.

But like everything in the swamp, nothing is as it seems.

I collect a few thitwhistle blossoms at peak maturity, tucking their violet heads into a small pocket inside my gathering bag. Buttoning the pocket closed, I continue my search for treasure. I find my namesake, a plant that will be in high demand this winter, and luckily there is plenty of it to harvest. I kneel before it, caressing the broad green leaves that match my hair, then the soft yellow petals that are a perfect match to the flowers growing in the mossy spots on my arms.

This plant is too old, so I look for another with younger leaves and subsequently, younger roots. I find a patch that is close to the water's edge and debate for a moment, then approach cautiously. First, I trim the leaves and put them in a magicked preserving bag, then dig the plant up and take its roots, careful of the thorns clinging to them. I place the roots in a different bag, one that is magicked not to tear. I do this with a few more plants, not wanting to overharvest but also needing to get as much as I can.

Today is Trading Day, one of the two days I actually interact with other people in the span of a year.

A ripple spreads through the water inches from my fingers and I swallow.

But it's too late.

A flash of fang is followed by a tremendous splash, then I'm pulled into the freezing water. A massive jaw frames my arm, firmly tugging but doing so in a careful manner, like a dog would do to a pup. Once I'm completely submerged, the pressure releases and I surface, sputtering. I fling hair away from my face, glaring at a set of bright yellow eyes. Vertical pupils watch me intensely and hundreds of cone shaped teeth compose the beast's smile.

Hundreds, no, *thousands* of scales compose the crocodile. Each individual piece meld together to form a glorious pattern reminiscent of an oil slick. The exact colors are always changing depending on how the light hits their scales, but the beast is usually a dark purple intermingled with electric blue. Their maw opens wide and a growl thunders out.

I roll my eyes, playfully shoving at their snout. "Fuck off, Hook. You got me all wet, *and* the plants."

"Don't be a dumbass. Next time you won't be so lucky." Hook chides, my familiar's deep timbre voice audible to only my ears. Not like anyone else is around, but if they were, they'd hear some nasty rumbling and grumbling that is completely crocodilian in nature.

My familiar gives me a gentle nudge towards the shore, snout to my back, and I climb back onto the floating island, sopping wet and mildly cold. I haul my gathering bag up into the grass, away from the shoreline, and spread my hands over it.

"Nesiga mayhim." I murmur, sighing when soft orange magick leaves my body and goes to work. Water molecules and the dirt brought with them wring out from my bag and its contents. The extricated water swirls in a glowing sunset of an orb over my hands, spinning lazily until I lob it over my shoulder. I grin when Hook roars, confirming that I hit my target.

Water magick isn't my specialty, but water likes me. I feel at peace with the aquatic roots that weave beneath the islands, and what are roots without the water that supplies them?

I stand and sling the bag across my chest once more, ensuring to give Hook a particularly dangerous glower. His eyes blink just above the water's surface, then disappear entirely. I blow out a raspberry, then continue on with my work.

Today is Trading Day.

I'm absolutely sure my home is not what most people would call grand, but I love it all the same.

Hook follows me there, sticking to the cloudy waters that lead to the largest floating island in Egret Marsh. Cypress and willow trees completely surround a small structure lofted into the air on stilts, still invisible from this distance. The sheer amount of fallen trees and vegetation swallowed by the swamp between here and there is enormous, and I've often wondered if there used to be a forest through here. I dodge and weave through a secret tunnel in the underbrush, covering my trail as I go. Threads of roots softly churn the earth, erasing what tracks I do leave for good measure.

"Have fun," Hook says, wandering off once he's sure I'm home, the bond between us quieting.

I snort. "Oh yes. *People*. Fun."

I pass through a familiar look-away ward, sighing in relief when I step into a small clearing, where the stilted house awaits. Strong, thick roots with rough bark form the pillars of my home's foundation. The roots forming the ladder and porch railing are thinner, but just as sturdy. Moss hangs from the surrounding ancient cypress in great curtains, further obscuring my home from view. Not that anyone visits the marsh, but if they did, they would have to look *real* hard to find my place. Just because my island is the biggest in the marsh, doesn't mean it's the easiest to access.

I cross the small clearing, relishing in how the soft grass tickles my toes. Everything is softer in my patch of the swamp, less threatening. Even the snakes are milder. I shift my bag so it's pressed against my back, then begin my ascent. Dirty hands and feet touch upon root wrought rungs. I climb for a couple minutes, taking my time. I'm not too proud to admit that I've fallen a time. Or two.

I pull myself up onto the wrap around porch with a groan, jingling the bells, bones and coins hanging from the open windows of my shack trimmed in white. There are multiple windows on every side of the house, each one remarkably different. Most were bartered for, or salvaged from the junkyard. A few I made and they didn't turn out *so* bad, just a little crooked. I made sure to paint them all white, though. The walls themselves are patched together at best, mostly sheets of painted plywood entangled with roots and thick bark. The roof is more of the same, perhaps more natural than man-made, aside from the solar panels.

The dark green walls, white windows and nature infusing my place in the world sets my heart at ease. I duck my head under the open door frame, telling myself *again* to just build a taller frame already. It was salvaged too, definitely not made for overtly tall fae. I shrug off my bag onto the round table inside the front room. A hall bisects the house, the front room rests on the left side and the right is divided between my closed off bedroom and washroom.

The front room is a combination of my reading area and the kitchen, *fairly* tidy if I say so myself. The only clutter to fill the place are the strange, now potted plants that I've found in the swamp and have yet to identify, along with my books. Bookshelves line the wall of the reading room opposite my cozy chair covered in blankets, but the shelves were long ago filled.

I make do, crafting leather straps which hang from the walls and hold half a dozen books. Plants hang from the ceiling in macrame nets that I made last winter.

Oh, don't forget the bones. Or the coins.

Marrow and metal hide in the nooks and crannies of my home, scavenged from the swamp and intentionally placed. To anyone else I suppose my place would *seem* in disarray, but everything is where it is for a reason. Sometimes I wonder what it would be like to have my things disturbed. It would be annoying, but that would mean someone was *here*.

I shake off the lonely thoughts and find a drink, then check the already prepared crates of dried skunk's cabbage leaves and roots, which is the majority of my inventory considering winter is coming. I have an entire crate dedicated to bags of aetherberries as well, they are *always* in high demand. As far as I know, the bog lining the northern edges of Egret Marsh is the only place the delicious, bright yellow berries are found.

It's one of the many secrets the land and I share.

There's jars of thitwhistles, mushrooms and radical healing moss, along with some knuckle bones for the more superstitious in Vieta. I've never met another *actual* witch, but I know there used to be quite the population in Levena before everything happened. I haven't been there since ... well, since the video store, and I have no plans on going back. Even if it is supposedly 'better.'

Kleo tells me every time I visit that *'there's a ton at Witch House, you should* really *meet them, Lys, I'm telling you.'*

And I tell her every time that I'm perfectly fine the way I am. What I *don't* tell her is that it's easier to be alone. I don't get hurt that way. What I remember of other witches is—well, not good.

While I have my garden and am pretty self-sustaining, there are still things that I need, or want I suppose, to live. Things like the supplies for my house, pots and pans, trinkets and books. I've collected quite a few things during my twenty years, despite the fact I only leave the swamp twice a year. During the AWO and NOJ's war on witches and magickal creatures, I only made the trip once a year. Those years were hard, and lonely.

That's thirteen trips thus far.

I make each one worth it.

Hook doesn't complain either when I bring home special treats like chicken feet or something equally weird, but whatever makes him happy. My companion insists he isn't lonely, but I feel like most familiars have much more exciting lives than he does. Nevertheless, I ensure to bring home stories, too.

The communal town of Vieta is much more docile than the metropolis of Levena, if not incredibly distant from the marsh. In the early years, the trip from here to Vieta would take at least a week on foot and what I could carry was limited, but then I was given a traveling stone by Gareth a few years ago, back when they were still illegal in the Northern Region. He didn't want anything for it, but I've still been trying to come up with the perfect thing to pay him back.

Between the traveling stone and my strengthening magick, the trips are more fruitful, and I can spend more time with my friends. For all my griping, the people of Vieta are rather nice. It's strangers I don't like, or trust. Last year I only visited in the spring, which is when I heard the news that witches were safe again. I didn't chance a fall trip, just in case. This will be my second trip this year, and I still have no intentions of visiting Levena.

After taking one last inventory, I clean up today's harvest and hang it to dry on the hemp line criss-crossing the open window over my sink. I duck into the washroom and clean up in the lukewarm shower, careful not to use too much water. The tank is getting low and I honestly don't feel like filling it right now.

I dress in another pair of high wasted pants, but tuck the pant legs into socks and knee high leather boots. I rearrange the necklaces on my pale chest, complexion freckled with spots of moss, sprouting blades of grass, and yellow flowers. Upon seeing the flowers in the mirror, I frown. I stare at them, debating on pulling the bright petals.

It's been a long time since I've been made fun of for them, and out here there's no one to tell me how awful I smell. I caress the soft, tender silk of a budding flower growing from my neck. If I pull the petals, the smell won't be as bad. Gareth, Nienna and Eilae have never remarked on my ... *scent*, but others might. Who knows what has changed since spring, who has moved there. My stomach twists uncomfortably.

I sigh, dropping my hand.

I shake my head, then go about combing back my bleach blond hair. Blinding locks interspersed with tendrils of spiraling green and budding broad leaves hang around my shoulders, the longest I've had it in a while. For a long time I thought it'd be better to cut my hair short, but I like it long. I don't wish that my hair was 'normal' anymore, either.

I smile at that, feeling a little better. Fuck people.

The edges of my burnt orange eyes crinkle upwards and I grin wider. The patches of soft green along my cheeks, forearms and stomach bristle with life, as if caressed by a soft wind. I leave the safety of my bathroom, shrugging on a flannel vest over my shoulders, leaving the buttons undone so my chest and necklaces are exposed. I don't get cold, not until there's a solid foot of snow on the ground. Even then, I only put on a sweater.

When I come face to face with the stacked crates, I call upon my magick. I put a hand out and whisper, "*Kul sheresh.*"

A net of thick roots conjures to life beneath the neatly arranged pile, rising and neatly wrapping around the stack. They tie off at the top, forming a pretty bow. I smirk, unable to help myself. Once the goods are secured, I take the small, metal chest sitting atop my kitchen counter. I open it, revealing three things. Three things that matter the most to me.

A traveling stone, polished amethyst in the shape of an oval.

A coin, worn and faceless.

A piece of paper, folded in on itself six times.

I hover over the parchment with shaky fingers and lungs, then draw back. I take the stone, then snap the lid shut. After putting the bomb back where it belongs, I stand beside a season's worth of work and firmly grip the netting. My heart thrums against its cage and I take a deep breath, steeling myself.

It'll be fine.

I'm immediately overwhelmed.

I land in a flurry of wind, soft orange light and a solid *thud*. I blink several times, acclimating to the incredible colors and light greeting me. Music, such heartfelt music, and laughter washes over my ears. My heart pounds at an odd rhythm.

Thump. Thump. Thump Thump Thump.

By the time I comprehend my surroundings, I'm overcome with dirty cold fingers and bare feet, gangly limbs and high pitched voices. My back hits the ground and I laugh despite the assault. Chants of *'Lysander! Lys! Lysander! It's Lys!'* ring through the air, bringing the music to a halt. Curious hands tug at my hair and I wince, but thankfully the group of hellion's parents rescue me.

Gareth says, "Kids! Let 'em breathe."

Eilae says, "Oy, Lysander! Long time no see."

Nienna says, "Hello Lys, you're just in time for second lunch."

I chuckle, pushing myself to my feet. One of the oldest helps me up, Martin I think? Honestly they have so many kids it's hard to keep them straight. I lay a hand over my heart and bow my head to the elves, noting a new face by their side. My heart thrums oddly again.

Thump. Thump. ThumpThumpThump.

"Hello, friends. I hope I haven't interrupted anything," I murmur, straightening. Not to my full height, considering I'm already twice as tall as everyone else when I'm hunched over.

Eilae scoffs, breaking away from her partners to hug me tight. "We've been waiting for you kid, it's Trading Day."

"Oh." I can't help but flush.

"Come, there's someone we want you to meet." Eilae demands, not unkindly, and I follow her, leaving the neatly packed goods behind. Eilae is a force of nature, so much unlike her comparatively docile partners, Gareth and Nienna. She's short for an elf, with blue hair shaved close to her head, big eyes just as vibrant. She's playful and blunt, but that's what I like about her. Eilae steers me over to where Gareth, Nienna and company are waiting in their little section of the backyard, surrounded by flower bushes and play structures.

Kleo stands with them, wildflowers tucked into her mismatched socks. It was one of the first things I noticed about her, and years later she still dresses the same. Patchwork overalls, sneakers and color. So *much* color. A knitted sweater lays beneath her overalls, all stripes and glitter. Her hair is longer than last time, shaved on one side with the remaining brunette locs cast over her shoulder.

"Hey Lysander," Kleo calls, grinning wide with sparkling hazel eyes. She doesn't run and embrace me like she usually does, and I'm assuming it's due to the ... witch, (oh my Gods, that's a *witch*) at her side. "Long time no see. This is Felix, my friend that I told you about?"

Thump. Thump. ThumpThumpThump.

My heart simultaneously explodes and fills with warmth. Yes, I've heard a lot about Felix. Every time I visit, Kleo talks and talks and *talks*, and it's usually about her *'friends back at Witch House.'* The people I swore I would never meet. That it would be *better* if I never did.

But I'd be lying if I said I'd never thought about them. What the witches were really like, if Felix was truly as good as Kleo said he was. If he was truly *'the best person ever, besides you of course, Lys.'*

The person I had built up in my head is nothing like I imagined, but infinitely *more*.

The man with golden eyes and infinitely long, tied back curls of bronze extends his hand to me. His small palm fits perfectly against my much larger one, and I *sigh* like a swooning idiot. To be fair, his tanned skin flushes a soft red, and his magick rushes against my fingertips for the briefest of moments, but it's enough.

He smiles, flashing white and slightly crooked teeth. "Hey, I'm Felix. It's nice to finally meet you, I've heard a lot about you."

And because I'm *me*, I say, "I'm not a skunk."

"*What*?" Felix raises a thick brow, a tenuous smile pulls at his lips.

"Umm." I choke, grip tightening around Felix's hand. He doesn't let go, and that smile *widens*.

Gareth says, "This is painful, right?"

Nienna says, "Shush, dear, this is a moment."

Eilae says, "It's worse than I thought it would be."

And because Kleo is the only one who is my *actual* friend, she says, "What he *means* is, the proper term for his fae lineage is *Lysichitum*, also known as skunk's cabbage, but we don't use that terminology here."

I remember myself and drop Felix's hand, then immediately shove my hands into my pockets and dip my head. Upon doing so, I remember that my flannel vest is unbuttoned. I fight the urge to button it, but then Felix says the most unexpected thing.

He says, "I thought so! Your flowers are so pretty," Felix chokes on *his* words and my head jerks up. He continues at a sputter, playing with the end of his ponytail. "We call them swamp lanterns, back at Witch House. Do you light up at night too? Can I touch your leaves? Oh my Gods, forget I said that, why am I still *talking* Kleo?"

I can't help but laugh, and he does too.

It's wonderful.

For a moment.

Then, Felix says, "Man, I wish Silas was here. I think you guys would really get along."

"Who's Silas?" I ask, noticing the exchanged looks between the family standing behind Felix.

Felix blushes furiously, the deep red extends down his throat and under the collar of his sweater. "Oh, he's my partner, another witch, like us."

Well, fuck.

Somehow, we manage to function like adults after that. Gareth, Kleo and Felix accompany me to the main hall, a longhouse centered in the town where Trading Day occurs. It's already full, considering I procrastinated coming here in the first place and the ... whatever the *hell* that was that happened back there.

I drop the net of goods with an unceremonious thud in the last empty stall, the sound lost to the noise of the crowded and upbeat atmosphere. Music flows from the head of the long-house, courtesy of some folk instruments. Kleo and Felix search for a table while I subtly call upon my magick, whispering words that untie the bow and retract the roots into the dirt floor until they're nothing.

"I'll find us all some food." Gareth claps me on the shoulder, smiling softly.

"Oh, okay. Thank you," I say, unable to refute him because I *am* hungry. I'm used to Gareth accompanying me, but not Kleo, and certainly not a man that I'm *pretty* sure is my everything and someone else's at the same time.

Quit being dramatic, Lys.

I sigh, flowers and leaves curling in on my body. Kleo and Felix fill Gareth's absence almost immediately, bringing over a long folding table. They set it up and I thank them, then get to work unpacking crates one at a time.

"Can I help?" Kleo asks, and I shrug. She and I set up one jar of each item on the table, leaving the extras in the crate. Felix studies each ingredient from the other side of the table, becoming increasingly excited as he evaluates my selection.

"Ooh, is that *hahlama* moss? Oh, and are those swamp lantern roots? Is that—" Felix interrupts himself, smiling nervously. "Sorry, I like plants."

Kleo scoffs. "That's an understatement."

I clear my throat, attempting to make small talk. "Yeah, you um, you run the apothecary in Witch House, right?"

"Yes!" Felix nods quickly. "Yeah, Calen and I do. They're better at the processing and preserving thing than I am honestly, but everything that comes before? That's my jam." He winces.

"Your jam?" Kleo teases, and he groans.

"That sounds nice. So, Calen's a witch too? I guess probably everyone that lives there is, right?" I chuckle nervously, giving my table one last lookover to make sure everything is out. Kleo watches us with a smug grin, standing at the end of the table between Felix and I.

Felix shrugs. "Not *everyone,* but Calen is, yeah. They needed a home, and Silas wanted them to come live with us, so Dad said okay."

My brain breaks. "Oh, that's—good."

Kleo takes off, muttering something about finding chairs and her sanity.

Felix comes around the table, tapping its surface as he does. "So, what about you? Do you live alone?"

I nod absently, burying questions. Questions such as; Silas invited Calen to stay as ... friends? Something more? If it is, then does that mean Felix has two partners? Or is it just Silas that has two? Have I gone insane and am reading into the smallest of things because of a—a *crush*?

"You alright?" Felix asks, standing closer than he was before. When did that happen?

"Yeah, totally." I fidget with the necklaces hanging around my throat, rubbing a coin between my fingers. *Totally?*

He chuckles, eyes dropped to my necklaces. "Okay. So, you live alone in a swamp, and only visit what … twice a year?"

That snaps me out of my stupor, but when I open my mouth, a customer arrives. I sell them a jar of … *swamp lantern* (because *yes* I like that term) roots, explaining to the faun how to boil them properly for a heat inducing tea. That is what most people use them for, the tea will warm their bones for hours upon hours, no matter the weather. Prepared into a syrup, the plant provides expectorant and anti-inflammatory qualities, perfect for respiratory issues.

After that, Felix and I don't talk much. Kleo comes back and word of aetherberries spreads, drawing people to my table like flies to a fallen fruit. They leave with so much more than they came for, and when Gareth returns, I'm almost sold out. A wave of calm washes over the longhouse as others partake in early dinner, the crowd ebbing. They eat six times a day here in Vieta, small meals that are filling regardless of their size.

Gareth and Kleo talk about the latest addition to her small farm that rests beside her parent's. Screaming goats.

"*That* sounds unpleasant," I mutter, and they all laugh. Even Felix, who has been quietly studying me for hours.

"And that is *exactly* why I'm offering sanctuary. Even the most … *obnoxious* things deserve love." Kleo declares, and I can't argue with her. I tell her as much, and she grins. "How's Hook doing by the way? I have his chicken feet ready."

I groan. "He pulled me into the water this morning, so his usual cheeky self."

"*Who* eats chicken feet?" Felix tilts his head, leaning forward in his chair across from me. Kleo and Gareth flank our sides, a tight circle.

Gareth chuckles. "That feisty croc. Still waiting to meet him."

I open my mouth but Felix's eyes widen, magick coloring them a soft pink for just a moment. He whispers, "A crocodile?"

When I nod, his whisper transforms into a shout. "You were almost eaten by a crocodile with chicken toes in its teeth? Oh gods, what if it said, *'mmm, you taste like chicken?'*"

Kleo laughs, face buried in her hands.

I laugh too, the moss and grass spots along my body grow in delight. "Hook is my familiar, he wouldn't eat me. But you're not wrong about the chicken toes, it gets to be quite a nuisance for him."

"Your familiar is a crocodile?" Felix balks, leaning back in his chair. He mouths, "That's so cool."

My cheeks warm and I shrug. "What's yours?"

Felix's excitement simmers down and he toys with the end of this ponytail again, which is loose now and half undone. "Haven't got one yet. Dad says that's alright, it'll happen when it's supposed to happen. He didn't get his until he was older, too."

"Oh," I say, unsure how to proceed.

Felix grins at me, releasing his hair. "It's alright. Tell me more about Hook."

And I do.

Later, after I've sold out and made some purchases of my own, after dinner when Felix tells stories about a man who was a mystery, and even a little while after that, Felix and I find ourselves alone.

I'm not sure how it happened. One moment Gareth, Nienna and Eilae, along with all their children and Felix and I, were sitting around a campfire and eating smores, debating how much to cook the marshmallows. Kleo and I were the only ones in agreement that they should be burnt to an absolute crisp, while Felix appalled me by only *warming* them up.

The galaxies are exceptionally bright tonight, and the double moons shine with a full, luminous intensity. The golden and silver celestial beings are centered overhead, physically at their closest to our planet. I love this time of year. It's colder here than back home at the marsh, but Gareth had loaned me a sweater, which I now wear underneath my vest. My necklaces rest atop the fabric, coins glint in the firelight and bones absorb moonlight.

Felix turns to me with a shy smile, we're sitting side by side on a log bench. Kleo had been right next to me, but she's gone, and so is Eilae, who was sitting on the other side of Felix. They're all gone. He gestures to my necklaces.

"You remind me of a crow," Felix says. I can't help but laugh, and he blushes. "I didn't mean it as a bad thing! It's just, they collect things, you know? There's a flock back home and they're always leaving the weirdest things around, not always shiny, but just ... random. One time, Marvin left me an acorn top with a piece of red thread pulled through a wormhole in it."

"How does that even happen?"

"Right? Can't very well ask them, considering Marvin's a crow, and *yes*, I named them."

I chuckle. "You're weird. I like that."

Felix laughs, finally taking the tie out of his hair, considering it wasn't doing much. "Thanks. I like you too, Lysander. I'm glad we finally got to meet, I've been wanting to come up sooner, but ... you know."

I shrug. "Yeah, I guess so. Better late than never, right?"

He nods, fidgeting with the hems of his sleeves. "Can I ... can I ask you a question?"

I stiffen a little, but say, "Okay."

Felix stares me in the eyes, his flash pink again. "Could you show me some magick?"

"*Oh,*" I whisper, then nod quickly. "Yeah, okay."

I clear my throat and stand, then sit back down, because I don't want to stand over him. He's already so much shorter than me, I feel like a giant just sitting next to him. He tentatively presses a hand to my arm, lips parting, and I startle. He pulls back, not taking his eyes off me. "Sorry, I didn't mean to make you nervous."

"Oh, I'm not. Nervous, that is."

Felix chuckles. "Okay. Well, you don't have to make yourself smaller, for me."

"Oh," I say, then stand and straighten to my full height before him. The leaves and petals in my hair and along my skin stand to attention, and I blush at the image of preening like a fucking peacock.

"Wow," Felix says, staring up at me with wide eyes. "You're really tall."

I almost lean down, but he takes my hand. This time, he doesn't let go. "No, don't." Felix stands beside me, my hand in his. I stare down at our entangled fingers, then back to his face. His neck is craned and it looks painful, but the determination in his eyes is almost frightening.

I squeeze his hand, then let go. I put my hands up, smiling wide. "Okay, have it your way, *tchotchke.*"

Oh, how he smiles at that. He pretends to be affronted, but that smile. It's perpetual, blinding. "I am *not* a small thing."

I shrug, turning away from him. I bring my hands to chest level and smile upon coming up with an idea. I close my eyes and murmur, "*Abracadabra.*"

For a split second, there's just the sound of leaves crunching beneath Felix's boots as he joins my side. An owl calling. A soft, chilled breeze rustling the small trees and flower bushes around us. Then, Felix's sharp intake of air when something groans thunderously beneath the trembling earth. His arm brushes against mine and my magick, it ...

It *spasms*, which is the only way I can describe it. The molecules riding my blood temporarily implode with power, with right, with *yes*. Then they expand with the feeling, fueling my heart with more energy than it has ever pumped before. A soft pink hue colors the edges of my vision and I sigh, fingers shaking.

Four pillars, each composed of eight thick roots, erupt from the ground softly, like how a plant sprouts and gently breaks the earth. The pillars rise to a height of about ten feet, then change direction and grow towards each other, weaving together to form a platform. As they do, smaller roots branch off the original eight. The foundations of the earth continue to diverge, split and grow together until a treehouse of sorts stands before us, a neighbor to the firepit.

A series of protection runes burn into the smooth, deep brown of the roots, temporarily glowing a bright orange until fading into the realm of invisibility. Although there are half-walls surrounding the porch of the treehouse, the spell will keep anyone from falling. Last but not least, a ladder unfurls from the upper level, its end hovering just above the ground.

Felix squeaks.

"Oh. My. Gods. That was ..." He side-eyes me, mouth work-ing open and closed. "Can we—we should test it out, don't you think?"

I grin. "Definitely."

And that's how the two of us ended up scurrying up a tree-house, squealing like a couple of kids. How the noise didn't wake anyone up, I'm not sure, but I don't care.

We flop inside the giant room of a treehouse, the root walls to our backs. I catch my breath through giggles and Felix does the same. He grins at me, golden eyes lighting up the small space between us.

"Show me yours," I murmur, and he tenses.

"Oh, that's *probably* not a good idea," Felix says, rubbing the back of his neck.

I wave around wildly, as if to say, 'Hello, treehouse?'

He groans. "Ugh, I hate the word for it."

I shrug. "So make a new one."

Felix blinks. "I totally should."

I elbow him and he gives me another shy smile. "Fine, fine. I'm a *Super Teleth,*" He waves his fingers dramatically.

I raise a brow. "Yeah, I've got no idea what that means."

"What?" He asks, high pitched. I give him a look, and Felix clears his throat, trying again. "Oh, that's ... kind of nice actually. Um, I can read minds?" His voice lilts and upon seeing my horrified face, more words spill out.

"Not all the time! I have wards up, you know? Otherwise that's ... a *lot.* I can move stuff too though, and talk with people telepathically, even if *they're* not a Teleth. I can tell how people are feeling too, just by their auras. The *super* part of it means I have more than one specialty. Or something like that."

"Wow," I breathe. "You're like a superhero."

Felix blanches. "Oh, please don't. I'm really not, and it can be annoying. I'd much rather have your awesome plant powers."

I shake my head. "No way. I can only control roots, not necessarily plants. That's boring compared to ... mind stuff! Have you ... read *my* mind?"

"No, no. I don't ever do that without permission."

"Oh."

"Did ... you want me to?"

I shift, our knees knock together and my heart does that *thing* again.

Thump. Thump. ThumpThumpThump.

"Yeah, okay."

Felix laughs, but it's shaky. "Nah, I probably shouldn't."

"No, really! I want you to. Only if *you* want to, that is," I say, cursing myself. I never talk, and I can't seem to *stop* talking around him.

"Okay. Just, put away anything you don't want me to see," Felix says, and it's quiet.

"Okay." I close my eyes. I try to clear my mind, which is an impossible thing to do.

"Are you ready?" He asks, and I nod.

I focus on Hook, and home. I picture the gardens around the house, the books on my shelves, the marrow and metal detailing my place. I inwardly chuckle at the thought of bringing Felix there, he'd really call me a crow then. A warm feeling settles in my heart and I sigh, thoughts turning to the places around the marsh I'd show him next. Silas too, if he wanted to bring him. And Calen, if that's ... if whatever they are to Felix warrants such a thing.

I tumble through thoughts, waiting for Felix to start, but all I feel is peace and questions and his pant leg crinkling against mine. I open my eyes and mouth, turning my head towards

Felix, but promptly shut my lips. His eyes are closed, a peaceful expression upon his face. A slight smile plays at his lips, and I swallow words.

Felix opens his eyes, golden irises focus directly on me. He murmurs, "I would very much like to visit your home. And if Silas and Calen are welcome, I'm sure they'd love it there too. It seems peaceful, beautiful. Thank you for showing me."

"Felix, do you ..." I start, then clear my throat. "Nevermind, it's not my business."

Felix smiles. "Yes, we're all together, *meira*, but Calen is only Silas', erm ... *romantic* partner, not mine."

"Oh," I say, unable to come up with anything else after hearing his endearment for me.

Light.

"I like you, too, you know. Your feelings were pretty strong." Felix taps his temple and I die a little inside, burying my face in my hands. "But we can't ... I have to talk to Silas, and maybe we could try being friends first? I'd like to be your friend, regardless of anything else. I feel like we ..."

I look up at him then. "What?"

Felix twirls a lock of hair around his finger. "I don't know. I feel like I already know you. Is that weird to say?"

"No," I shake my head immediately, heart racing. "My heart does this weird thing around you."

Felix blushes furiously. "Oh."

"I want to be your friend too, Felix."

Felix smiles then, my words effectively erasing his nervousness. "Okay, let's be friends."

A few more hours pass in the treehouse and dawn is a very real threat. I'm not sure if I've ever stayed awake this long, but I don't care. I soak up everything that is Felix, and he wants to know everything that there is about me, too. I tell him about being left behind at the video store. He tells me he doesn't remember being left behind, but he remembers the bruises.

We lay on the floor of the treehouse, heads together. He's absolutely delighted by the fact that *yes*, the parts of me that are plant glow softly under the moonlight streaming in through the open windows, like a lantern.

He asks, "Why did you tell me you weren't a skunk?"

"I went to school for a little while, after they left me, before things got ... bad. Everyone, even the teachers, would comment on how I smelled. It was a distraction to the class and I–I spent a long time hiding because of it. I," I sigh, drawing the breath from my toes, "I used to pull my petals out, because it makes the smell not so bad. But I don't do that anymore."

"I'm glad that you don't," Felix whispers immediately. "For the record, I like your flowers, and I like the way you smell. You smell real, like earth and spring and Dad's pot."

I bark out a laugh. "That's amazing."

"I know."

I ask, "What's your Dad like?"

And he talks and talks and talks.

Hours after saying a reluctant goodbye to Felix and promising that I'll send him a letter, I lay atop the roof of my home and watch the sun come up. Warm rays of purple, pink and gold wash over the marsh, thawing the frost my swamp suffered last night. I flip a large coin between my knuckles, a new addition to my collection. Its golden hue matches that of the man's eyes who gave it to me.

Felix had said, "If you ever need Witch House, say the words and someone will answer. Dad gives these to witches in case of emergency, but you can use it for communication, too. You're part of the family now, whether you like it or not, swamp witch."

And oh, how I smiled.

Here

And

Now

I lay in bed, watching him sleep.
I kiss his lashes, wondering if I'm dreaming.
I breathe, and he breathes.

A Goat and Four Kids

Thatch
Two Days After Returning

A heavy weight pounces on my chest and an ungodly scream rattles my brain.

I bolt upright, gasping for air.

Darkness blankets my vision and everything is cold, so cold. Phantom claws scrape brain matter against my cranium, leaving behind gouges filled with screams and terror. My ribcage heaves, desperate for something, *anything* to fill my quaking lungs.

Warmth starbursts between my shoulder blades, comforting and grounding and *home*.

Air hitches in my throat and I grasp onto it for dear life, stuck in the dark.

He, *Him*, The One I've Waited For, says, "You're safe, Thatcher. You're home, and I'm right here. Do you want me to hold you?"

I gain ground across a slowly evaporating battlefield, forcing my body to reconcile with itself. Centimeter by damned centimeter, my eyelids shutter open. It makes no difference, even after waking up in the same place more than twice, I don't recognize my surroundings.

I focus on the hands before me.

Two are pale and freckled, shaking violently as they grip fistfuls of a flannel blanket. In the distant reaches of my mind, I understand that these are *my* hands.

Another is dark and upturned, revealing a steady palm that is inches from my own, waiting patiently. He, Him, The One I've Waited For, it's *his*.

Right there, I only have to reach out and take it. I want, no—*need* to turn my head and look upon his face. It's in his soulmark, reality is. I have to make sure.

That beautiful mark never shone in my nightmares.

I *need* to see it.

He says, "I'm here, love. Right here."

I stare at my hands.

I break a sweat doing so, but I manage to slide my pinky over just enough to brush against his hand, which is all I can manage.

But it's enough.

His fingers entwine with mine, bridging our skin and the energy bubbling beneath. His magick flows into my exhausted spirit like a warm syrup, peaceful and right. His firm grip is unrelenting, purposeful and necessary. I hold onto him with all I have, while my other hand releases the blankets in slow increments.

A shuddering breath makes its way in and out of my lungs. Then another. And another.

Eventually, my spirit takes hold of reality, too. My body convulses as if visited by a ghost, then slumps. The fingers on my back slide to my shoulder, pulling me into a firm side. "Is this okay?"

I manage a nod, and my head is beyond heavy, but the relief that comes with regaining my body outweighs the exhaustion. Slowly, cautiously, I tilt my face up. Air escapes against his neck and jaw in short pants. This close, the vibrant beacon on his face nearly blinds me, and I welcome the sensation. I finally find his soft eyes cast in a simmering green, evidence of his magick coursing through me.

Arlo smiles.

My heart settles into an easier rhythm than the one it struggled with before.

"There you are," He whispers, squeezing my hand. "Do you want to try going back to sleep? It was just Pesto, he's gone now."

I shake my head, and if I had half a mind I would've giggled at the goat's name like I have every time I've heard it thus far. I bury my face into his neck, bone tired, but my mind is wide awake. Both his arms wrap around me now, pulling me into a heated bare chest. I sigh, inhaling everything that is Arlo.

Paint. Coffee. Ozone.

He pets my hair, humming a soft tune. He doesn't ask questions, just allows me to be. Many things have changed about Arlo during the years we've been separated, but some things are exactly the same. I focus on sliding my fingers through the hair on his chest, skimming over ink and muscle.

A soft chirrup rolls from the corner of the room, a snowy owl perched in a literal tree. I stare at the beauty, turning over the story Arlo told me about his uniquely named familiar. Narrowed pale yellow eyes stare right back at me, quiet and calm. A breath shudders through me once more, then I feel a little bit better. Peeking through our nest of entangled limbs and blankets, I slowly absorb our bedroom.

It's not the same room I left him in eleven years ago without so much as a goodbye. This one is larger, an airy studio that takes up the entire second floor of 'Dad's Cottage.' The furniture has been brought over from the bedroom we briefly shared before, the bed we lay in now is the same one we made in love all that time ago. We haven't left since that first day filled with talking, kissing and holding.

Sleep claimed the entirety of yesterday, or is it still today? I'm not sure, but I do know I've never felt so tired after returning. It's as if my body has finally accepted the fact that we are staying for a while.

But all this sleeping, interrupted only by aftershocks of panic and trauma, has left little time for any substantial conversation. The first day was the most we've talked, and I wasn't exactly able to absorb all the ways my soulmate's life has changed. Not to mention I do believe he's restraining all the bad things that happened during the time I was gone, sugarcoating what he has to. I don't recognize most of the people he talks about, and there's a tiredness to his eyes that wasn't there before. I know Arlo wants to show me everything, but he's patient.

Always patient.

"Why do they *all* call you Dad?" I ask, voice thick with disuse.

Arlo chuckles, continuing to play with my hair. "Caspian started it, of course. I decided early on that I wanted the kids to have their own space, and at first it was just Felix, Silas and I, but it didn't take long for others to find their way here. It took a little bit, given the state of things, but bit by bit we worked on the place, when we could."

Arlo sighs, a silent lapse in his story that says everything, and nothing.

"He kept saying things like, 'Well, let's go work on Dad's house,' just to be a dick, but then everyone else started saying the same thing, and calling me Dad. I didn't mind it, not really. Felix though, it only took him a few months. I think he was nervous or something, but—"

Arlo clears his throat and I can practically hear the blush overtaking his face. "It was nice to know he truly felt like mine, because Gods, these kids ... they're everything to me, you know?"

"I know," I laugh a little, but it comes out as more of a breathless sound than anything. "It's in your nature to be fatherly, and I knew you would do wonderful things with this place." I shift down, laying my head on his stomach. I listen to his gut rumble, and he runs a hand up and down my back, fingers riding over my scars. There's many new ones there, disrupting the road map he briefly knew so long ago.

I don't mind that he can see them. He doesn't mind that they're there.

"I'm so proud of you, my *leva,* such a life you've built here. And the kids, I do want to meet the rest of them, they sound—"

Arlo chokes on a bellowing laugh. "I'm warning you, they'll be the death of us, but they're ours, and we're theirs."

I gasp, a whispered and shuddering thing that I cannot hold back.

"I mean, if—if that's what you want. I'm kind of a package deal now, in case you didn't notice." Arlo adds, voice low and teasing, but there's a waver to it as well. The wind shifts and the house creaks. His body rises and falls beneath mine with purpose, like he's preparing himself for the worst.

I press a kiss to his stomach, leaving a promise there before resting my cheek on his skin once again. "Of course, Arlo. I wouldn't have it any other way, but I don't ... I don't expect any of them to care for a man they just met, certainly not as a father. Felix even, he's changed so much, little shit." I add the last part under my breath, thinking about how he and Silas ran away from me in the woods.

Arlo chuckles, and I could listen to his laugh in the dark for eternity. "They're all little shits, but they have such big hearts, love. Give it time."

I smile against his skin. The darkness in my mind retreats even further, not welcome in this little moment of promises and happiness between us. He breathes with purpose, then again, like he's working himself up to something. When no words follow I turn my face, pressing his belly to my other cheek. He's watching me with a tender expression, eyes returned to their natural golden brown.

"What?"

Arlo's lips push together and his brows narrow. A second passes, then his face softens again when he speaks. His soulmark briefly alights. "I have so many things to ask you."

I smile, and it's easy. "We have all the time in the world."

He smiles too. "This is true."

"You may have one question. Two if you're lucky," I tease.

He nods, silently running his fingers through my curls. They're longer than they used to be, down to my shoulders now. I cut them every week during the time I was gone, until the last year of my absence. I wanted this, him petting my hair.

"How long was it for you?" Arlo asks, a barely spoken thing.

"Hmm," I say, trading cheeks on his stomach again. The room is blanketed by moonlight, shadows of heavy snowflakes dance across the soft green walls. The sight reminds me that I will experience snow in Levena again, for the first time since its founding. My heart beats faster at the memory of that day, one of the happiest ones I have.

"Do you remember the men from our date, the bard and his lover?"

He palms the back of my head, fingers threading through my curls. "I do."

"I spent a year with them, or at least what a year is there, in a world quite like this one but—different. Older, but the people there aren't like they are here. After helping them, I spent ... fifteen years? in a place that was *nothing* like here. There was no magick, no magickal creatures. It was dull and gray, sickly. Devoid of people. After that, I spent three years on an underwater world, and that one was the trickiest of the three because—"

"You spent fifteen years alone?" Arlo asks, chest stilling after the strangled words escape.

I wrap my legs around his thigh, heat washing over my neck as I cling to him. I hate it when he leaves in the morning, every moment that we're together I find myself blanketing his body with mine in some way or another. "I was, at first. But that was my mission, to revive the planet. It's not empty anymore, and the magick is back—"

"You ... *repopulated* an entire planet?" Arlo asks, stiffening further beneath me. My heart quickens, anticipating him to be angry and have come to the wrong conclusion.

But because he's Arlo, he laughs.

And a few other snickers join in, leaking through the crack in the bedroom door. Four sets of *very* conspicuous eyes hide in the dim hall on the other side. Silas' voice is anything but subtle, although I think he's trying to be. "A planet full of red headed disasters, imagine that?"

I can't help but laugh. A real one, pulled from the depths of my gut and thick with delirious happiness. We both sit up, Arlo's arms wrap around my waist and he kisses my shoulder. He tries on a stern tone, but it's a miserable attempt. "Children, eavesdropping isn't welcome in this house."

"Finish the story! Just pretend we're not here." Calen whisper-shouts, their round face on the bottom of the pillar of heads now poking through the door. Silas is above them, long white hair tickling the top of Calen's beret. Felix is hoisted onto Silas' back, grinning wide with his hands hooked around Silas' neck. Lysander stands behind them all, the swamp lantern fae is tall enough to watch the scene unfold with calm curiosity. I only briefly met him and Calen the first day I was here, if fleeting waves count as anything.

Arlo gives me an imploring look, a brow raised and lips hooked slightly upwards.

"Well, it was most certainly *not* what you're thinking. Genetically that would be a nightmare, could you imagine? No, I—oh my, there's no way to say this without it sounding smug, is there?"

I glance between the young folk in the door and Arlo, fingers twisting in the blanket. I don't have to parse through my words anymore, or at least not for the reasons I did before. Truth comes easily now, but stringing coherent sentences together still isn't my strong suit.

"I *made* everything, with magick. I modeled that place after this world, at least in the sense it's populated by humans and magickal creatures both. The geography there is entirely different from here. I don't make any world quite the same."

And ... *silence*.

Oh sure, there's gears turning behind dilated eyes and cheeks flushed red with excitement, and perhaps anger, because blatantly meeting your potential maker is not something everyone experiences. Our secret was a secret for a reason. I know this now. I've seen the consequences. *Anukai* were never meant to be revealed.

And I know now how much Arlo and I have fractured the universe by revealing the God's greatest kept secret. How long until the ripples of consequence splash across us, is another question.

It's Lysander who poses a question I've never been asked before. Then again, I've never actually *told* anyone the extent of my power. With the butter yellow flowers along his freckled skin glowing softly, he asks, "Why didn't you make people good?"

For a few moments, I contemplate the best way to answer. Calen watches me with big orange eyes half-obscured by vibrant peach and pink colored curls. Silas and Felix are now sitting on either side of Calen in the threshold, Calen's wings are wrapped around each of them. The door has found its way mostly open and Lysander stands directly behind Calen, an odd expression on his face. The sprouts in the mossy spots along his bare arms curl in on themselves, wilting under my silence.

"Understand that what I'm about to tell you is a secret, hm? You clever lot have discovered many things here, but there are more secrets than you can ever imagine. Some are best kept to a whisper, for the Gods are not always forgiving." I give Arlo a pointed look, then wait for affirmative nods from our guests before continuing. "What I do is like ... have you ever played with clay, or mud even? Made little figurines?"

All four nod again. Arlo is a solid weight behind me, his arms warm and tight around my middle. His breath fans across my neck steadily and in the space between his mind and my own, an even pulse beats firmly, insistently. The connection between soulmates is not an instantaneous thing, but rather something to be nurtured and built. While our thread is firm and unforgiving, time has worn its surface.

The thought briefly crosses my mind that Silas and Calen, Felix and Lysander, their bonds must be golden and silver chains constructed of the most love and trust that anyone could muster. A tinge of jealousy follows the thought, then is swept away by graitude that they all didn't have to wait ten thousand years before finding their soulmates.

"When a world is born, someone like me can create life using the ... *clay* of the universe, if you will. But these new lives, flora or fauna, are empty shells until the Gods fill them with spirits of their choosing, both old and new souls. A new soul is born neither good nor evil, they just *are*, I think. It's everything that happens after we're born that defines who we are, for better or worse. I don't make those decisions. I am only a designer, and there's more than just I who puts things into motion, I assure you. And after that initial birth, there is little need for someone like me to create more life, and the clay is used up anyway. Until the cycle starts all over again."

"But why?" Lysander asks, hands balled into fists. "Why can't someone like *you* choose who is allowed to walk the earth? Stop bad people from coming back?"

"That's too much power for one person to have," Felix says, reaching up to take Lysander's hand. The fae stares down at Felix as he takes his hand, holding onto Felix like he's a lifeline. During one of my periods of consciousness intermingled with the haziness of dusk, Arlo had told me that the four of them are usually inseparable, that Felix and Silas both found their soulmates in other people, but they found a way to make it work between them.

I didn't ask Arlo how that made him feel, if he wishes that something like that would've happened between him, Caspian and Tobias. I don't even know how he feels about Caspian anymore. It's then that a sudden and gut churning thought comes to me.

Did Arlo ... *love* anyone else, while I was gone?

Could I blame him if he did?

I was gone over a decade, and while I don't know the specifics I do know that there was a war that involved a back from the dead Leon and not one but *two* hateful groups that tore apart Levena and feasted on its carcass. I know that Arlo kept everyone safe, but who kept *him* safe? Who comforted *him* after a day of fighting and death and loss?

Certainly not me.

We promised each other that we would wait, and I did. I was completely alone for more than half the time I was gone, and I found good company in the world of fae, but nothing even remotely close to love, to desire or anything neighboring it.

"Some things aren't meant for us to know," Silas says, interrupting my thoughts with an answer that I should listen to. He's got an arm slung around Calen's waist, the demon is nestled into his side and yawning in a manner that reminds me of the silver feline currently laying belly up in Silas' lap. Opal, Silas' familiar.

"I think that's a bullshit excuse for the Gods to get away with whatever they like. *'It's for your own good.'*" Calen mimics through another yawn. "Besides, it sounds like they're taking all the credit for *your* work. Someone who does everything you do *should* be a God."

I smile weakly at all of them. "Perhaps you're all right. Or maybe it's not up to the Gods, either. Maybe it's inevitable to have good and evil, and everything in between. We can't appreciate true love and goodness until we've seen how dark it can be. Or maybe that's bullshit too, I don't know."

"And that's how I know it's time for bed," Arlo says, causing a collective groan to escape from his kids. *Our* kids?

"What do you mean?" I ask, and he chuckles.

"You swore, love."

I huff indignantly, crossing my arms. Felix chuckles and gets to his feet, as do his partners. "We'll see you tomorrow, Thatch. Night, Dad, love you."

My heart swells instantaneously.

Calen and Silas repeat the sentiment, while Lysander switches out Arlo for Dad. He's only been here for about a year if I remember correctly, and he doesn't stay at Witch House during the spring and summer. He seems quiet and reserved, even perhaps wary of me.

"We're taking Pesto with us," Felix says, poking his head back in the bedroom a few seconds later with an armful of goat. The salt and peppered pygmy goat with a marvelous beard chews on the string to Felix's hoodie, but the witch doesn't seem to mind.

"Get your beauty rest, love you." Arlo calls after them, and then it's just us again. I lean into Arlo and he falls back on the bed, taking me with him. Voices bounce through the downstairs, muffled and excited. Pesto screeches once more, but it doesn't terrify me this time, then the front door opens and shuts.

"Were they here when we fell asleep?" I ask, and he chuckles.

"No, they were chasing after Pesto who really did *not* want to leave Felix's last harvest alone, and clever thing that he is, ran in through the cat door. Hence the whole goat jumping on your chest ordeal."

"You have a goat and four kids," I yawn, cuddling into his side, right underneath his armpit. "Not to mention all the other kids who think of you as an additional parent to the ones they've already got."

"You gave birth to a planet. I think we can call it even." Arlo murmurs, full of bright amusement.

"I suppose we can." I laugh onto his skin, then press a kiss to his ribs. "You're not surprised?"

"Oh I am, but what am I to do? I'm in love with a God."

"I'm not a God," I murmur, nipping at the muscle shivering beneath my touch.

He inhales sharply, then takes hold of my chin. Arlo directs my gaze up to his, glittering and full of love. "But I can worship you like one all the same."

Calloused hands move with tenderness and love, guiding me into his lap. My knees settle on either side of his hips, and my palms fall upon his stomach. He's outwardly softer than before, a broad veil that hides the strong muscles beneath. Curling peppered hair trails from the hem of his trousers, up his stomach and chest, then thickly pools at the hollow of his throat. I follow each fiber with the pads of my trembling fingers, and he watches.

He watches me recommit his body to memory for the hundred time since returning. We've kissed and touched and held and *loved*.

But we haven't had sex.

He hasn't asked and neither have I. It hasn't felt ... *right*, not until now. When my fingers settle into his beard, one that is much shorter and neater than my own, he sighs in relief. His eyes flutter shut, his breathing evens out when I scratch my nails across his jaw. A smile blooms across my face as I watch him relax under my touch.

And just like that, he's asleep.

I chuckle, continuing to play with his beard and ignoring the fact my cock is hard. His is too, an echo of the sleepy erections that have rubbed against me in the early morning.

But I haven't wanted it until now.

I lay on his stomach and repress a groan from the near painful sensation shooting through my groin. I wrap my arms around his sides and sigh, wrinkling my nose as his chest hair tickles my face.

Tomorrow. Tomorrow I will leave the house. I will tell Arlo I'm ready for him to show me around, introduce me to his family—*our* family.

And tomorrow night, I'm going to seduce Arlo Rook.

Secret Heart of Hearts

Arlo

A maelstrom thunders in my ears and I'm out of bed before my mind fully catches up. A bodily green glow surrounds my figure as I sprint down the hall leading from our bedroom to the stairs. I search the bond between Thatch and I, finding that he's in the house. An eerie quiet greets me as I hurry down the spiraling steps, and the stench of burnt *something* assaults my nose.

My heart jackrabbits out of my chest when I reach the landing, having to duck under a thin layer of smoke. I cross through the front den at a slower pace, making my way towards the kitchen hidden at the back end of the cottage.

"Thatch?" I call out, unsure what the hell's going on.

"Don't come in here!" Thatch shouts, and after a seconds-long pause, adds, "Not that I'm doing anything, it's just … my hair! Yes, my hair, a complete mess!"

I glare at the smoky atmosphere in disbelief. His hair. *Right.*

A stampede comes around the corner of the narrow archway leading to the kitchen, resulting in Felix and Lysander standing before me. Oliver skitters around the corner, nails sliding until the golden canine crashes into Felix's legs, knocking his knees out. Of course.

"Go back to bed!" Calen yells from somewhere behind them, followed by grumbling from Silas. I'm pretty sure the word 'disaster' was somewhere in there.

"We've got everything handled," Thatch adds stridently, *clearly* in distress.

I raise a brow at Felix who hides a snicker behind his hand, then slide my gaze to Lysander. "Do I want to know?"

"They're fine." My son's soulmate shrugs, but his cheeks pinken and the tiny white flowers growing in delight along his cheeks give the man away. "You should probably go back to bed."

"I—"

Another ear shattering noise just like the one that awoke me echoes throughout the cottage, a sound I belatedly recognize as pots and pans falling to their death. I open my mouth and take a step but Felix and Lysander charge forward, each hooking an arm under my armpits and followed by Oliver.

"We're going for a walk!" Felix calls over his shoulder to the miscreants in the kitchen.

"Come back in twenty minutes for a definite *not*-surprise!" Calen bellows, and I allow myself to be dragged away only because the faintest giggle follows me out of the cottage, one I've missed for so long.

Once we're back at the stairs, Lysander and Felix drop me unceremoniously. The wreath of evergreen fir, pinecones and magickally preserved sunflowers hanging on the inside of our front door catches my eye, Lysander's gift to me. I was sworn to secrecy about its origins, but everyone knows how big Lysander's heart is. "Get dressed," Felix orders, gesturing to my trousers before leaning down to whisper conspiratorially. "We're going Yule shopping."

I grin and hurry up the stairs, just as fucking excited as the kids waiting for me. My fingers ride the cherry banister the entire way up, leaving behind good luck magick for the next person that does so. I turn on a light switch upon coming to the top of the stairs, illuminating the endless framed memories resting on the walls. Decades worth of photos hide between hanging plants, intermittent bookshelves recessed into the walls, and canvases.

All painted by my students.

The doors on the right side of the hallway lead to Thatch's library, the war room, and a guest bathroom, while the left side holds two guest bedrooms and my studio. I stand before the library door for a moment, staring down at the shining door knob that's locked more than it is open. I'm hoping that will change soon, the fact that Thatch is out of bed has me ready to do all the things, *show* him all the things.

But I want him to set the pace. I want him to take control.

I shudder at that thought, and "Dad!" breaks me out of my trance, like Felix knows *exactly* what I'm thinking. He can control his magick much better now, but he doesn't need it for me. He knows that I can get lost easily, all without moving.

"Be right there!"

I don't waste time in the bedroom, not even to make the bed, although leaving it a mess makes my eye twitch. I have no idea where we're going, but I put on warm underlayers beneath my jeans and a sweater knit by Gowan. One of the last she was able to make before her hands got bad. It reminds me of the sun, of Thatch. I look over to Dewdrop's perch, she's sleeping for the day. The snowy owl keeps close to the island, only staying in the house during daylight hours. I smile looking at her, but then my old leather jacket catches my eye, draped across the back of a chair at the vanity table. Thatch laid it to rest the first night we went to bed together, and he hasn't picked it up again since. I think about the adventures he must've had in it, and I wonder how it survived after all this time.

I doubt it fits me anymore.

Gingerly, I pick it up. Warmth radiates throughout my fingers, and when I bring the leather to my face, flashes of energy from the places he passed through before returning home dance across my cheeks. It hits me like an exotic and heady drug, a magick that doesn't belong in this world but is magick all the same.

I slip my arm into the left sleeve. Electricity dances across the tendons in my wrist.

I slide it across my shoulders, right arm into the sleeve. Light shoots straight into my heart.

I sigh, exhaling a weight that I've held onto for so long, I had forgotten it was crushing me. I dip my nose into the collar, smiling when I find nothing but cedar and campfire. The wrist cuffs have worn from where Thatch slid his hands into the sleeves, gripping the edge and worrying the leather between his thumb and fingers.

My heart hurts to think of him alone, worried. He's strong, so strong. I know this.

But the thought of him being alone for so long kills me. I had our family. A family I don't think he feels a part of, yet. We've included a ghost for years, telling his story and keeping his memory alive so thoroughly that even those like Lysander, those who never met Thatch, know what he was like.

Is like.

I lace my boots up, slide on a rusted orange beanie that matches the sweater, then leave behind my worries. Today is a new day. Tomorrow is Yule. He's here, I'm here. We're all here, together.

I hope that it's enough.

Because deep within my secret heart of hearts, a worrisome thought has festered for years. This life is enough for me. This little life full of children, the changing of the seasons, magick, little cottages and a little herd of animals, not to mention the occasional danger.

How could a life like that ever be enough for a God?

When Felix said let's go for a walk, I didn't expect he meant through a half-frozen swamp. Then again, I should've known better.

I follow behind him and Lysander holding hands and talking in hushed whispers. My own hands are buried deep into my jacket pockets. I've only been to Lysander's place a couple of times, the first I was accompanied by him and his partners, but the second time it was just us. We talked for hours, tin roofing to our back and nestled high into a tree of roots he long ago brought to life himself.

It was then he told me how long he'd been living in the swamp, alone since he was a young child. Like many of the others living in Witch House, he was abandoned when the AWO and NOJ began the Witch Hunt. A sort of kindred spirit formed between us, unspoken and quiet like the fae himself. I'll never forget the day Felix came home after visiting Kleo's family farm, near silent and completely unlike himself.

He confessed what he found to me first, saying, "What do I *do*, Dad? I *love* Silas, I *love* him. But when it was time to leave, Dad? I felt like my heart was being *ripped* out, and I can't let him go. He smells like your pot, did you know that? Lysander thinks it's awful and I think it's *everything*."

And I had said, "Be honest with Silas. He loves you, and you love each other enough to decide what's right for you both. And I think you're forgetting you've been through this before, with Calen. You told Silas you loved him no matter what, and that you could make room for Calen too.'

Felix had looked at me with such worry in his eyes. 'But what if it's too much? What if I'm too much?"

We hugged, and he cried.

Two days later Silas dragged Felix back to Vieta, berating him for leaving his soulmate behind. A fellow witch no less, and how *dare* he not bother to introduce him to the rest of us?

I chuckle as we step into the clearing that Lysander's home hides in, and Felix looks over his shoulder questioningly. "Thinking about the day you brought Lysander home for the first time."

Both boys —-no, *men*— blush instantly. I watch their fingers tighten around the other's hand. "It was a good day," Felix nods, staring up at the man taller than I. Lysander looks down at him with such fondness it makes me want to abandon my mission and find Thatch.

"It was," Lysander says, dipping his nose down to brush against Felix's.

I wander ahead and allow them a moment of privacy, watching Oliver take off deeper into the swamp, to find Hook no doubt. I turn my face to the sun that isn't enough to ward off the chill and bone nipping wind, but is enough to make me smile.

That fades, though, the more I think about Thatch.

I think about Thatch awaking from his nightmare and into a panic attack, not just last night but the night before as well. How he stirred every time I had to get up, grasping at the place I had once been. How his eyes crinkled with groggy worry, not closing with relief until I assured him I'd be back later.

How he hasn't left the cottage since arriving.

How everyone has been asking to see him, and then worrying when I say he's not ready.

They ask, 'What happened to him? Where's he been? Is he okay?"

And to be honest, I don't rightfully know, and I should. A wave of guilt washes over my heart and before it can drown me, a steady hand rests on my shoulder. I startle, finding Felix beside me. He gives me a small smile, taking my hand in his. A smile that says he knows exactly how I'm feeling.

"Ready, Dad?" Felix asks, and my lungs seize. I fold him against my chest, wrapping my arms around him as tight as I can muster. He doesn't fight it, he hugs me back with just as much force as I'm using. "What's this for?" He asks, muffled by my jacket.

"I'm happy that you're mine, Little Witch. That's all."

Felix snorts. "You always get so emotional around the holidays."

I shove at him, messing up his hair. "There's nothing wrong with being sensitive."

And that starts a rough-housing match that Lysander has to break up from his vantage point on the porch surrounding his elevated house. He watches us with mild amusement as I beat

Felix to the ladder, leaving behind some magick for him to slip on.

Of course, messing with a Teleth is always a *great* idea because he just picks the ladder up whilst we're both on it. This leads Lysander to call upon roots deep beneath the frost layer which bring forth a thunderous sound, cracking open the earth. The roots cling to the ladder, securing it so neither of us fall to our death, and I reach the top first.

I pump my fists triumphantly and Felix isn't far behind, but he doesn't wallow in his defeat. He grins at me, and that's how I know he's planning his revenge for later.

"We're running out of daylight," Lysander says, leading the way to his front door, one he has to duck under. We reframed the doors on Witch House after he came, and I don't think I've ever seen anyone smile so hard from simply walking through a proper door frame.

"It's not even nine yet, chill your jets." Felix mutters, earning a glare from Lysander.

"You know I hate that phrase," The fae says, switching on lights as we pass through the narrow hall that divides his small house into left and right sections. "Anything you like Arlo, just let me know."

"Don't tell him that," Felix says, and I chuckle.

"You sure you don't mind?" I ask, to which I receive an affirming grunt from the other side of the house, which admittedly isn't very far. I take my time, smiling as I study Lysander's collection of bones, books and metal which hides in the wall nooks, on shelves, and on every other available surface. "I could spend days looking over your collection and find something new each time."

"Crows, both of you," Felix says, plopping down on a velvet couch that exhumes dust. He picks up a book at random and starts reading. I join Lysander in the kitchen and take a seat at the dining table, watching him slowly fill its surface with different trinkets that he had stashed away.

Three things catch my eye.

A cloak pin. Thin copper wires are braided together, then wrapped around the original ring. The pin is simple, a spiral at the end holds a small garnet that needs to be polished. Thatch doesn't *own* a cloak, but I can imagine him snuggling up into one easily enough.

A ring with a circular emerald inset into the middle, surrounded by silver rays of sunlight. It's also simple, but the craftsmanship is breathtaking and reminds me of us. I've never seen him wearing any jewelry, but my gut tells me he'd like it.

Lysander watches me closely while I puzzle over the first two items, then leans back in the chair he's taken up while I study the third. A large, pillar candle scented like fir and *clean*. Magick, old and barely detectable but there nonetheless, seeps into my trembling fingers.

"It's a Neverlight," Lysander says, drawing my attention. "They never go out on their own, and the fire will never spread. I'd been saving it for emergencies, in case the solar panels failed, but ... I don't really need it anymore. Take it."

"Are you sure?" I ask, staring back down at the candle in my hands. I wonder if it would help Thatch during the night. He insists on leaving the lights off so 'he doesn't bother me,' but maybe I could convince him to put this on his side of the bed.

On his side of the bed.

"Positive." Lysander frowns at Felix who is lounging upside down now, still reading. "Need anything *tchotchke?*"

Felix grins. "Nope, all good."

Lysander opens his mouth and almost looks as if he wants to argue, but then shakes his head and picks up his things. When I offer to help he waves me off, so I tuck the candle into an inner pocket of my jacket and wander over to Felix. I sit on the floor so his head is level with mine, and he glances over at me.

"He'll like it."

"You think so?"

Felix dips his chin once. "I know so."

I look to the now empty kitchen, Lysander has disappeared into his bedroom. "Everything okay?"

Felix grins, and it's so sudden and blinding that my heart instantly overflows. "He doesn't like surprises."

I smile too, remembering the day I took Felix Yule shopping, which was a few weeks ago now. Felix had drawn Lysander from the generous pot of names. I declared long ago that our family is too big to buy a present for each person. I lean closer to Felix and whisper, "He'll like this one."

Break His Hip Birdie

Thatch

We stare at the burnt carcasses of cinnamon buns, my third attempt at fucking *breakfast* of all things lies in the snow, lifeless and pathetic. Silas' head is tilted, eyes narrowed on the cinnamon buns like they've personally wronged him. Calen rubs their chin, lost in thought.

I sigh, tugging my hood around my face before gesturing towards Silas. "Okay, maybe I will take you up on that offer now."

Silas laughs, but it's not unkind. "Oh no. You're making breakfast, and it's going to be epic. But maybe not cinnamon rolls."

I bury my face in my hands, groaning. "Today is a disaster."

"Nonsense, you can't declare that until after noon." Calen pipes up, smiling. That seems to be their usual expression, and I don't mind it.

I glance at Calen, fingers parting from my eyes. "Says who?"

Calen grins wider, fingers hooked into their denim overalls affixed with numerous bright patches. Tino, their ferret and familiar, rides shotgun in the overall's floral chest pocket, nose poking over the hem. Calen's great leathery wings puff up a little bit. Silas puffs up a little too, standing behind Calen and staring at their wings with reverence, like it's the first time he's seen such a thing. I'm quite sure that it's not.

Calen says, "Arlo, of course."

I chuckle, unable to help it. That definitely sounds like something he'd say. "Alright. Let's try again."

"Now that's the spirit!" Calen agrees, leading the way back inside. Silas walks by my side, tapping his left thigh and staring at Calen's tracks left behind in the few inches of snow we have. The back door is still open, but now that most of the smoke has evacuated the cottage, I shut it behind us. Opal weaves between my feet, greeting me like she did upon coming in with Silas earlier. A much less wet and excited introduction as opposed to Oliver, but I quite like the dog's energy.

"How do you feel about baked toast?" Calen asks, peering into the fridge.

I exchange a look with Silas who takes a seat in the nearby breakfast nook. He shrugs with a little, knowing smile, then takes to petting Opal when she jumps in his lap. I steel myself and come round the large island situated in the center of the kitchen. Pots and pans, the ones that tried to *murder* me earlier when I only needed *one*, hang overhead on a rustic rack of iron and wood. Big round windows overlook the backyard, strands of dried citrus slices hang in the morning sun. The entire cottage is a mixture of rustic vintage and bizarre artistic flair, and I love every bit of it.

I had spent an hour this morning exploring, trailing my fingers over every nook and cranny in the home Arlo built for us.

You would never know that I haven't lived here, my most prized paintings that I had left behind in the bunker decorate the den and the walls of the upstairs. There are bookshelves in the den, but my personal books do not line any of them. A few of my three dimensional puzzles, wooden and otherwise, rest on the round coffee table centered in there. I quite like the den, there is a blazing hearth and a pretty woven rug anchored by the coffee table. The curtains pulled over round windows are tasseled and woven with the brightest threads, just as eclectic as everything else in the house.

I had spent a long time in the chaise lounge though, the one by the windows. There are well worn depressions in the cushions where perhaps a hip and head rested for far more many nights than they did in the person's own bed. There's a knitted, striped blanket folded neatly at the foot of the lounge, and I had brought it to my face and inhaled every sleepless night Arlo ever had in this room. Then, ever so carefully and neatly, I refolded the blanket and placed it back in it's spot, wondering how many times Arlo did the same.

"Thatch?" Calen calls, breaking me from my thoughts.

"Sorry." I shake my head, putting on a smile. "In case you don't remember, my first attempt at this was eggs, which, well ... I'm glad Pesto at least was able to enjoy them." I pointedly glance at the goat in question, waiting patiently by a ceramic bowl that is neatly labeled 'Pesto' and situated nearby Silas. The goat cocks his head, eyes narrowing at me like he's planning something nefarious.

Silas laughs. "Sorry, but Pesto will eat anything."

Calen claps twice, grinning. "I've got an idea."

"Oh?"

They nod, removing their beret which reveals two short horns veiled in peach curls. They toss it to Silas, then roll their sleeves up. Calen and Silas exchange a look, then Silas nods once. I watch as they remove their phone from a pocket, curiosity winning out over my frustration.

Within a few seconds, music spills from the device. It's airy and light, a fast paced violin accompanied by more string instruments and bells that are decidedly festive. The sound is so ... *real*, as if the band is right in the room with us. Calen sets the phone down on the counter beside me, then extends a hand, eyes glowing with sunset magick.

I chuckle nervously and slide my palm into theirs. Calen takes my other hand and rests it on their waist, and belatedly I recognize this for what it is. A dance, Calen is leading me into a *dance*. Stars, when was the last time I did *this*?

With Arlo, I had told him I couldn't handle loving and losing him.

My breath hitches, but that's all the sadness my heart is allowed before Calen quite literally sweeps me off my feet. They are marvelous, erasing my disadvantage that is unfamiliarity with such a simple act as dancing. The notes seem to swirl around us, no—*through* us— and I laugh. It starts off small and unsure, but then Calen is laughing too, spinning me in circles upon circles in the middle of the kitchen. Tino squeaks from Calen's pocket, and something tells me it's with genuine *delight*.

Silas calls out over the music, "Don't break his hip birdie!"

And it goes on and on, the laughter and music and *sun*.

Sunlight streams in through the colored mosaic of windows overlooking the backyard, casting reds, blues, golds and purples onto our moment in time. Calen's soft cheeks burst with happiness when Pesto joins in, prancing around us on those little hooves. A breeze moves through the room, bringing with it the distinct scent of wet earth. I stumble to a stop and nearly topple us both over, but thankfully Calen keeps us upright.

Lysander, Felix and Arlo stand just inside the backdoor, bringing snow covered boots and flushed smiles with them. Felix grins wide at me, stands on his tip toes and gives Lysander a kiss on the cheek, then practically throws himself into Silas' arms. Silas takes it in stride, situating the witch across his lap and burying his face into Felix's chest.

And Arlo—oh my stars, *Arlo.*

He's looking at me like I'm something.

Like I *mean* something.

Like I exist.

Like this is *it,* this is ours and he's mine and I–

I run to him.

How could I not?

It's like the first day of my new life all over again. I kiss him, and kiss him, and *kiss* him.

He laughs against my lips, big palms settling on my cheeks. His hands are so cold, but I don't mind. I don't mind at all. His fingers slide across my jaw, tangling themselves into my hair. Heat courses up my spine when he opens for me, allowing my tongue to find his. The same thought that occurs every time we kiss swims in the background.

Can he feel how much I've missed him?

The solid, fast paced rhythm of his heart that matches every beat of mine proudly affirms yes, yes, *yes.*

Someone clears their throat, accompanied by Felix whistling and Calen giggling. The music tapers off to nothing and Arlo pulls back, one hand traveling to my waist to keep me from going anywhere. He grins, eyes glittering with hazel delight. His soulmark is infinitely bright. "Good morning to you too. Your hair looks lovely, by the way."

I flush instantly, a hand going up to the curls in question. "What do you–*oh*, that. Yes, well, obviously I was lying before.

I was trying to make us breakfast, and … well after a few failed attempts, we somehow ended up dancing."

Arlo chuckles. "Calen's solution to everything." He gently knocks my forehead with his. "It'd be nice to cook together, don't you think?"

I shrug, absolutely sweating now. I glance over to the breakfast nook where the four witches are seated together now, stretched across someone else in one way or another. They laugh and talk in hushed tones, I don't doubt that they're listening in.

"I wanted to do something nice for you, but I'm not very good at this." I admit in a whisper that strains my throat more than I care to admit, unable to meet his gaze.

Arlo captures my chin gently, turning my attention back to him. He's smiling softly, and there's no pity like I thought there would be. "But you tried anyway, for me. You have no idea how much that means to me."

I roll my eyes, but that only makes him smile wider. "You're not a hard man to please, Arlo Rook, that's for sure. Fine, but only because it's almost lunchtime now and I'm starving."

"It's only ten," Silas corrects me, and Felix immediately stands upon realizing the moment is over. Arlo and I separate, but he doesn't leave my side, taking my hand in his.

Felix bounces back and forth between his toes and heels. Calen's at his side, brimming with just as much excitement as he is. Felix says, "Dad, let's show him how to make *lechem*."

I glare at Felix. "That sounds difficult."

"You got this, I promise," Felix says matter of factly, and it's hard to argue with the jut of his chin and the daring look in his eyes.

"And where are you two going?" Arlo asks Lysander and Silas who are halfway out the back door.

Lysander says, "Checking the woodstove," at the same time Silas says, "Making sure Witch House isn't in shambles."

Calen squeals. Felix grins. Arlo glances at me with ... worry? Why is he worried?

"We'll be back in twenty minutes," Lysander says, then takes off after Silas who didn't wait to hear the rest of the conversation. Opal stays behind, following Oliver into the den across from the kitchen. Arlo sighs, shaking his head.

"Something wrong?" I ask, and he flashes me a thin smile.

"No, not at all," He glances at Calen and Felix who have already started gathering ingredients and other things in the kitchen, then back to me. Arlo takes my hand and leads me out of the kitchen and into the backyard, shutting the door behind us. Wordlessly, he guides me to the snowbank where my failed attempts at breakfast lie, then lets out a heavy breath.

"*Leva*, what's wrong?" I ask, taking both his hands in mine.

"Nothing's wrong," He shakes his head. "I'm a blunt man, and I'm too old to not say what's on my mind, so I'm just going to do it. I'm ... worried." Arlo flushes, staring down at our hands. He squeezes, and I squeeze back. I want to ask *why*, but I give him the room to speak when he's ready, like he does for me.

"It's loud here, busy and chaotic, and ... small? Thatcher, you're *everything*, quite fucking literally. And I don't—I can't wrap my head around the fact that you're *here*. You could do anything you wanted, and you chose to come back to *this*. Is this good? Is it still what you—"

"Oh Arlo," I say, because I can't let him go on anymore. This time it's my hands on his face, grounding him to the earth. "Of course I came back. You are my *home*, this is the life I want, *you* are what I want. That's not ever going to change, because you are my *sanity*. You asked me if I was alone during all that time? No, I wasn't. Because I had you, always you."

Arlo Rook, legendary Hedge Witch and Protector of Witches in the Northern Region, a title I learned through Calen, breaks in my arms. He falls to his knees in the snow, face burrowing into my stomach and arms wrapping tightly around my waist. He has stood for over a decade against forces I don't fully understand yet, but it's *me* that brings him to his knees.

That just won't do, so I kneel too. I hold him to my chest, ignoring the cold seeping into my bones. I breathe, eyes closed and chin resting on his head. I tell him, "I'm here,"

And, "I love you, Arlo, why can't you comprehend how fully entangled in my heart you are?"

And, "I'm not leaving. Not ever again. Try and make me, I dare you."

And he laughs and *laughs* through the tears.

A short time later has found us back in the kitchen, accompanied by softer music pouring from Arlo's phone this time. Felix and Calen are here too. My eyes are swollen, irritated by the corpses of past tears, but Arlo's solid line of warmth at my back makes the discomfort worth it. His chin rests on my shoulder, his back must be killing him to be hunched over like this, but I'm certainly not about to ask him to move. It smells like bread and warm and evergreen.

"Good, just like that," he says, driving every hair on my body to stand up on end.

It's taken flour in my hair and syrup on my shoes to achieve an acceptable dough, and when I finally *did* get it right I had to start all over again, due to Pesto scampering into the kitchen to scream his fool head off which led to *me* screaming, then throwing my dough through the air. He dutifully gobbled it up, then took off like nothing happened.

"I hardly did anything." I glare at Arlo from the corner of my eye, my fingers resting on the loosely braided *lechem* that somewhat resembles the perfect one Felix braided in demonstration.

"Sure, love." Arlo chuckles, kissing me on the temple. He does straighten then, reaching into his pocket to retrieve a wildly ringing phone. He silences it, frowning.

Felix perks up from what must be his sixth loaf, we ended up making enough dough for an army. He and Arlo exchange a look, but then Arlo shakes his head. Felix rolls his eyes, and I wonder what exactly was said between them. Calen giggles from their place at the breakfast nook but otherwise stays out of the silent discussion, writing furiously in a small notebook.

"Is ... everything alright?" I ask, glancing at Arlo whose phone starts ringing again almost immediately.

Felix chuckles, earning a scowl from Arlo. "Fine, Kitty is just being annoying," Arlo says, giving me a tight smile.

"Oh," I say, staring down at my flour dusted hands. I look back up to him. "Do you ... is this how you normally spend the day before Yule?" I laugh weakly, shaking my head. "Nevermind, that was a silly question."

The seconds-long silence that follows is too much, and thankfully Calen breaks it. They're standing beside Felix now, smiling. "Actually, it is. We spend the day before cooking the things that will keep well, like the braided loaves. Don't think we made extra just so you could practice, they'll get eaten up." The demon winks, and I can't help but laugh a little.

"Oh, well, that's good then."

"Well, if you guys have this under control," Felix claps his hands on his pants, brushing away some of the flour. He playfully pushes Arlo out of the way, then pulls me into a quick and rough hug. I'm so taken aback by it that I don't have time to return the embrace. He moves on to Arlo, promising him that he'll take care of *'it.'*

Then it's just us.

Arlo chuckles nervously, rubbing the back of his neck. His lips open, but I beat him to it. "*What* is going on?"

He waves vaguely, turning his attention to the oven currently full of pans. "Nothing, it's nothing. People are just ... asking about you?" His voice verges towards high pitched and I can't help but smile a little. Of course I hide it behind a hand, but he's facing away from me anyway. "Okay, asking may be a *gentle* term, but it's just because they've missed you. Kitt especially, but it's really not a big deal, whenever you're ready, you know?" Arlo finally glances at me over his shoulder then.

I cross the room leisurely, hands twitching at my sides. My heart pounds when he faces me and I'm more than a little nervous, but I try not to let it show. "I think that'd be just fine, dear. I'd like to say hello, and you all celebrate the holidays together, do you not?"

His shoulders loosen and a large palm trails along my arm, cupping my elbow. His other hand captures my wrist, and he greets my palm with tender lips. Against my skin he says, "We do, but I want you to be comfortable."

"I'm not fragile." I snap, and I'm not sure where it comes from.

His fingers entwine with mine, and he nods. "I know."

"*Good.*"

He chuckles a little. "Great."

I narrow my brows at him. "I'm serious."

"I *know*."

"I don't remember you being this infuriating."

And he laughs then, loud and sudden. "Trust me my love, you have only seen the surface on how *infuriating* I can be." He leans close, dropping his lips to my ear. His next few words are nothing more than whisper, a stark contrast to the firm grip he has on my hand. "But you'll be begging for me to deliver just the same."

"Oh, I don't know about that," I murmur, sliding my fingers up his chest. I lean forward and press a kiss to the hollow of his throat, overcome with a heated and satisfied smile when he shivers. "I have a feeling you'll be the one on your knees, dear."

"Is that so?" Arlo asks, chest heaving against me. His fingers thread through my hair and his chin rests atop my head. "I ..." He laughs, pressing a kiss to my curls. "I have nothing to say, you've bested me."

I stare up at him, grinning. "Good, it's about time you learned your place. Now, call your friends, invite them over. Then we'll move some of this bread over to Witch House, yeah?"

Arlo grins sheepishly. "Funny thing, that. The Misfits are already over there, have been for a little bit now. Sure you're ready for the wolves?"

Always a Circus

Arlo

Thatch's eyes widen and his lips part, releasing a singular, "*Oh.*"

I wince. "*Yeah.* Today is kind of the day that the Misfits and everyone else gathers at Witch House to celebrate Yule, but I didn't want you to feel like you *had* to come, I know you haven't been feeling well."

He straightens, jaw flickering. "You're telling me that while I've been burning cinnamon rolls and you've been playing in the swamp, everybody else has been—*what*, waiting for us?"

"Not *really*," I say, tone rising in pitch. "I told them we wouldn't be coming."

Thatch raises a brow, and I shrink a little. "You really think that any of your family would let us hide away during a *literal* holiday? It's *your* house! We're going." He takes my hand, leading me upstairs. I open my mouth but he keeps on berating me, and I can't find it in me to be upset. It's kind of adorable, his tirade, so I listen with a hidden smile.

"Oh no." He stops suddenly in the hallway leading to our bedroom, and I nearly crash into him. He whirls around, hands flying to his curls. "I don't have any good clothes!"

I cup his face in my hands and kiss him.

He glares at me.

"Just because you haven't seen your closet, doesn't mean you don't *have* one. How would you know what clothes you have? I've been fetching them all for you, Your *Majesty*."

"Jackass." He swats my shoulder playfully, trying incredibly hard not to smile.

I gesture for him to continue, most definitely watching him go. He catches me looking, throwing an eye roll over his shoulder. We stand in the center of the bedroom and he spins in a circle, brows furrowed.

"I don't see a closet in here, there's only the bathroom." Thatch gestures to said room, which I enter without a word. It's large enough for a tub and toilet on one side, while on the opposite wall is a long vanity which houses dual sinks. On the end wall is a door which leads to our shared walk-in closet, something Caspian insisted we (Thatch) needed. How Thatch missed it I'm not sure, but then again he has been in a fog for the past couple of days. A rectangular, plain mirror hangs on the wall over the sinks, and it has stopped Thatch's pursuit of me.

I look over my shoulder to find him staring at himself in the mirror.

I swallow thick emotion and stand behind him, resting my hands on his hips. He pays me no mind, and I watch his eyes flicker across the reflection, scanning himself from top to bottom. He's wearing light jeans and a hoodie of mine, all black with the hood pulled up and sleeves covering his hands. Thatch chews on the inside of his cheek, holding his breath as he does. I lean down and press a kiss right behind his ear, nosing his hood out of the way.

He sighs deeply.

"I haven't changed much, have I?"

I laugh.

Hurt and confusion plays across Thatch's reflection, so my outburst is short lived. "*Oh*, you're serious," I say.

"Well of course I am," Thatch says indignantly, trying to turn away from his reflection.

"Hold on." I keep him still and he glares at me in the mirror. My right hand leaves his hip, slowly, and when I'm sure he won't pull away, my fingers rise to his face. I swipe a thumb over a scar on his chin. "You didn't have this the last time we met."

My left hand rises to his throat, pulling down the color of his shirt. "And there's a freckle here I haven't kissed yet. Play in the sun much, did you?"

Color spreads up his neck, blooming across his cheeks. "Perhaps."

I chuckle, stepping around him until we're chest to chest. I take his hands in mine, thumbs brushing over his knuckles. "Your hands are rougher, and this little sunspot is new." I turn his right hand over and kiss a thin line that marks the heel of his palm. "This scar."

I straighten, finding his face has softened immensely. I release one of his hands to thread through his curls. I twirl one in particular around my finger. With a conspiratorial grin, I whisper, "And I hate to break it to you, but you're turning silver, too. We *both* are."

"What?" He utters a single word, spoken with so much trepidation and fragile hope that it breaks my heart. I nod, releasing him. He makes his way to the mirror like a ghost, leaning over the counter's edge to get as close as he can. Thatch twirls the curl I had captured moments before, staring at it in the mirror.

He stays like that for a long time, unmoving except for his eyes.

I wonder about many things. Did he avoid mirrors before, or what he would find in the reflection? I know that Thatch and his body do not get along. I had initially thought that it was his scars that bothered him, but now I wonder if there's something else to it as well. My heart aches for him.

I join his side and gently rest my palm in the small of his back. He startles, lips parted and eyes glistening. I ask, "Are you alright, love?"

Thatch nods, huffing out a small laugh. He wipes his eyes with the back of his sleeve. "I'm not a vain man, I swear it, but ... I *have* changed, haven't I?"

I lean down, kissing his temple. "Yes, and now we get to change together. Come, let's get you some clothes."

He blinks rapidly, then shakes his head. "Right, the celebration. Well, I'm not the only one who needs to get changed."

Thatch gives me an appraising look and I grin. "You can dress me in whatever you like. Hell, you could tie me up in a bow and I'd be fine with that. Well, probably not for the gathering, but you know what I mean."

Thatch snorts. "You are terrible at this."

I smile, because he's smiling too, now. "I know."

"I can't believe you, we're going to be *late*." Thatch mutters, straightening my tie for the third time in the past two minutes. We're standing in the foyer and he's fidgeting, procrastinating, but I don't call him out on it.

"*There*, that's better." He exhales, giving the crimson fabric a final tug before smoothing his hands out on his dress slacks. I realize that I'm staring and silent for far too long when he tilts his head back, brow raised and a quirk to his lips. "You alright there?"

I nod, then press a kiss to his forehead. "Perfect. Are *you* alright?"

He chuckles, fingers twisting in my waistcoat. "Is it that obvious?"

"Only a little." I brush curls away from his face, then cup his cheek with a steady palm. I won't tell him that we don't have to go, because I don't want him to think that *I* think he's fragile. I want to respect his wishes, but I also want him to be *okay*. "We can't stay long, though. I'll need your help at the shop tonight, if you don't mind."

Thatch brightens immensely, eyes widening. "You mean, it's still ... even through—*really*?"

I can't help but smile at his sputtering excitement, despite the fact my heart weeps for the person who helped keep Thitwhistle's —and me— alive while Thatch was gone. A wave a guilt washes over me and I clear my throat. I'll tell him about ... all of *that*, later. He's smiling, and I don't want it to go away. "We did have to close down for a few years, but only to the public. Thitwhistle's saved many lives during the Hunt."

"A place didn't do that, you did," Thatch says immediately, surprising me.

I shrug. "I wouldn't have been able to without it, or this place. And if you want to be *technical*, I wouldn't have had either without you, so in a way, you saved Levena. *Again*."

Thatch blushes immensely, nose wrinkling. He opens his lips, brows furrowed and mouth filling with something I don't want to hear right now.

I lose myself. Time. Thought. It's only for a moment.

But it's enough.

I take his face into my hands with an unrelenting grip and crash our lips together. He *oomphs* against me, clutching my waistcoat even tighter. I belatedly think that everyone will know, they'll see my wrinkled clothes and they'll *know*. I sweep away his deflections with my tongue and hold onto him with everything I have. Magick surges through both of us with terrifying amounts of force.

One wrong move, and it all blows apart.

I replace my tongue with words, keeping his lips trapped beneath mine. "When I pay you a compliment, you will accept it as truth, for I am no liar, Thatcher Gaillot. You are worthy of honesty and kind words, and I will shower you with them until the day I die. Make no mistake about that, my love. Do you understand?"

He breathes, pupils replacing iris.

And I breathe.

Thatch nods, lips and nose brushing against me. He exhales, "Tell me again."

I tell him.

I tell him that he matters.

I tell him that I love him.

I tell him that he is worthy.

And I tell him that I am no liar, Thatcher Gaillot, make *no* mistake about that.

He pulls away first, cheeks flushed, eyes wide and ginger lashes wet. He smiles, blinking up at me innocently whilst patting my chest. "Well, since that's ... *settled*, we best get going."

Then he turns on his heel and throws open the front door to our cottage, effectively leaving me behind in the dust. I sprint after the sly fox and throw him over my shoulder, which causes both of us to laugh and laugh and *laugh*. He hits my shoulder, half-hearted shouts for me to put him down ensue.

Somehow, he ends up on my back with my arms hooked under his knees. He rests his chin on my shoulder and sighs, arms loose around my neck. "I like it here, with you."

My heart fills. "Yeah?"

"Yeah, Arlo. I really do."

"I'm going to remind you of that sentiment after this is all said and done." I tease, gently setting him down before the back door of Witch House. Both panels of the dutch door are shut and the curtains are drawn over the windows, shutting out the intense sun while it hits its peak over our little island. The enchantments surrounding the house are successfully keeping the sure to be raucous noise inside to a minimum, making it seem like nobody is home.

But I'm sure there's *dozens* of people on the other side of those windows, peeking around the curtains to get a better look at us.

Thatch chuckles, hugging my arm to his chest. "I'm excited, but you'll have to help me with names. I know you've told me about everyone, but ...."

Not everyone. Only the people who are living.

"Don't worry, I'll be right here," I pat his arm which is tightly hooked around my left bicep. "The whole time."

He smiles. "You will?"

I nod. "I will."

Before I can take the first step towards the door, Dewdrop lands upon my right shoulder in a flurry of white and mottled black. She's awake early. Thatch's eyes go wide, and a slow smile blooms across his face. Dewdrop tilts her head, golden eyes focused entirely on him. "Oh, hello. Dewdrop, is it? Pleasure to meet you."

Dewdrop evaluates my soulmate for a moment more, then dips her head. Clutched in her talons is a sprig of fir, dusted with snow. I take it from her, heat warming my cheeks. *"I like him,"* Dewdrop relays in the space between our minds, outwardly silent as she straightens and ruffles her feathers.

"I knew you would, thank you for this." I reply, gently rubbing my cheek against her wing. With that, she takes off for an early survey of the island, washing us in a heavy gust of chilled wind. I give my attention back to Thatch. "She's happy to have met you."

He bounces on his toes a little, face breaking with joy as he watches her go. "Wonderful, absolutely wonderful."

I swallow, looking down at the evergreen in my hand. Magick and I are one and the same, calling upon it doesn't even require the use of hand conjurations or words most of the time anymore. I turn the sprig over in my hands, conjuring a pin on the backside of the small thing.

"Come here," I say, pulling his attention from the sky. He stands before me, a gust of wind kicks up some snow from the cottage roof and sprinkles throughout his hair. "Courtesy of Dewdrop, mind if I?" I gesture to the lapels of his waistcoat, and he nods.

He watches me fumble with the pin, biting back a smile as I work. "It's a sign of hope for the future, did you know that?" Thatch murmurs, and my fingers pause.

I give him a lopsided grin, then continue the damned puzzle of a pin. "Oh, really?"

"It's true, I swear it."

I finally manage to get it, then smooth out the lapis brocade of his vest. Thatch is always handsome, but dressed in the well-tailored dress slacks, white button up, and the intricate waistcoat, he's a vision. "You're incredibly handsome tonight, Mr. Gaillot."

He smiles wide, tries to stop it, fails miserably. "You think so?"

I kiss him fiercely, then leave Thatch just as quickly as I had come on to him. "I *know* so."

His eyes flutter open and his lips close, reluctantly. He glances at the house, then back to me. "Well, we should go before they break the windows, don't you think?" He gestures to the fluttering curtains, and I chuckle.

"Notice that, did you? Well, lead the way, my love."

He does, resting trembling fingers on the doorknob, his other hand grips mine firmly. I brace myself for the sounds of a crowd gossiping and shouting.

But nothing comes.

Instantly my mind rushes to *wrong*, but my gut tells me nothing is amiss. Thatch pulls me inside, and we enter a silent and organized chaos. The collective space is known as the Big Kitchen, dimly lit by candles hovering around at various heights. In the usually empty center between the 'Food Kitchen' and 'Witch Kitchen' are the long buffet tables we use for gatherings, filled with endless dishes and platters clashing in color and style.

The outskirts of Big Kitchen are blanketed with people and familiars. Most of the time, familiars do their own thing, but during the holidays they prefer to stay nearby their witches. Witch House can get crowded with all the feathers and furs in addition to people, but that's why we made it bigger. Plus, they're all well-behaved. *Mostly.*

Tobias, Caspian, Marlena, and Zeke are the closest in the circle to us, standing to the left of the door now shut behind us. Tobias opens his arms and Thatch flies into them, laughing. Words meant just for the two of them are murmured, then they separate with wide smiles.

"Scarlet," Caspian extends his hand to Thatch who takes it without pause, giving him a firm shake. "Good to see you again."

Thatch flushes, the color plain to my eyes even under the dim candlelight. "Thank you, it's good to be back." He says hello to Marlena, then introduces himself to Zeke who is practically brimming with excitement.

Kitt and Lindsey are next in the circle, both descend on Thatch with hugs and squeals the moment he comes their way.

Felix, Lysander, Silas, and Calen are standing together, arms entangled around each other. Miles and Lily stand to their left, Ramsis sits atop Miles' vibrant sweater covered shoulder. Jo, David, and Serena stand to the right of my son's group, accompanied by the rest of Calen's orignal pack. Thatch gives every single person his full attention, introducing himself over and over. Everybody says the same thing to him in one way or another.

"We know, we *know*, we've been waiting, and we're so *happy* to have met you."

Gowan, Iris, and all four of their children are next, shedding moss and flowers as they embrace Thatch and welcome him back.

Doc hugs Thatch so tight that Thatch's back cracks, despite the fact that they never *actually* met, last time. Doc's human wife, Ilisia, shakes Thatch's hand and wishes him a Happy Yule.

And Kleo.

Kleo breaks from the mass of her family that she stands with, throwing her arms around Thatch's neck. She embraces him with all the force in the world and he lets out a little *oof*, hugging her back with the biggest smile on his face.

Quentin and Elochian are next. Quentin and Thatch hold onto each other for a long time, and Loch surprisingly gives Thatch a hug too.

And it goes on, and on. I stand by his side through it all, squeezing his hand when he finds me and letting him go when he's swept up again. Helena and Rhea surprise him, as do Bob and Ren. The young residents who sought refuge in Witch House after Thatch's time welcome him just as warmly as those who have met him, each one thanking him for his hospitality. He gives me a knowing look every time, and I wink at him in return.

Last, but not least, is Dusan.

Silence and love is thick in the air as the two embrace, the only sound is their joint tears falling and soft murmurs not meant for us. Felix catches my eye and he taps his temple, his silent request for permission to enter my mind. I nod.

"Was that okay? Thought a quiet entrance would be better than, well, you know. The usual hurricane theatrics."

I smile at him. *"I should've known this was all your doing. Thank you, it's just what he needed."*

Felix nods, then Miles says something and draws away his attention. I watch as Felix listens, the orc gestures to where Thatch and I are standing. Felix grins wide, glancing over at us. Thatch joins my side, interrupting my people-watching. Like the tide going out, the circle breaks and people disperse in a soft and chattering wave, flowing out of Big Kitchen and into the rest of the house.

Thatch tugs on my sleeve, ears red. "Um, Arlo?"

"Yes, love?"

He rolls his bottom lip between his teeth, and it *does* things to me. He pushes out a breath that lifts the tussle of curls resting over his right eye. "I'm *really* hungry. Can we eat now?"

I laugh, brushing away those pesky curls that I love so much. "There's snacks, but you'll have to wait a little bit longer for dinner."

Thatch groans. "Having a massive meal at two in the afternoon does *not* equate to dinner, Arlo. I don't understand this—this, bizarre notion!"

"Speaking of food, did you guys remember the *lechem*?" Felix pops out of the crowd moving around us. Lysander stands tall at his side, absently stroking between Oliver's ears.

I groan. "No, I did shut them off, but I'll go back over—"

Lysander shakes his head. "We got it, come on *tchotchke.*"

They take off, Thatch snickers whilst watching them go. "How many times a day do you all go back and forth?"

I roll my eyes at him. "It's quiet most days, believe it or not."

"*Don't* believe it, it's always a circus here." Caspian interjects, joining us. He lifts a plate of rolls from his lap, offering them to Thatch who gleefully takes two. "But that just means there's good entertainment."

Thatch chuckles over a mouthful of bread, and something in my heart settles at the sight.

It doesn't take long for us to be whisked further into the horde of people, or for said people to forgo their initial restraint and pepper Thatch with questions. We end up on different sides of the gathering, but not *too* far from each other. I keep an eye on his relaxed shoulders, watching for tension. His face is bright and eyes crinkled, a wide smile plastered across his face as David shapeshifts into a reindeer before the God's eyes.

Because no matter what he says, that's what he is to me.

It's nostalgic and peaceful, wholesome and right.

I twist the leather cord on my left wrist, sighing. Wondering how the *hell* to prepare him for dinner. When that piques my anxiety, I switch gears and think about him above me last night, straddling my waist. Time passes and my heat skins with every goddamn second. I can't get my fucking head out of the gutter. Every time Thatch laughs or runs a hand over his beard, I'm shoved deeper into hypotheticals and fantasies.

'I have a feeling you'll be the one on your knees, dear.'

"Arlo, I swear to the fucking *Gods* if you don't get your pheromones under control, I'm going to throw you out the window."

I choke on a mouthful of candied walnuts, sputtering like a fucking lunatic. Doc and Ilisia howl and laugh at my plight. Thankfully Gowan has my back, offering a glass of water which I take advantage of immediately.

"You guys are awful." The fae chastises, rubbing between my shoulders soothingly. Her littlest, Dandy, clings to her leg while his siblings wreak havoc somewhere else.

"Everything okay?" Kitt calls from her place beside Thatch in the Den, and I give her a thumbs up. The Den is a catch all space that functions as a meeting area, living room, and study. It used to be the dining room that sat opposite the kitchen, but since Thatch was last here it's been enlarged and repurposed, like the rest of the house.

The dining table we fucked on over a decade ago rests in my house, now.

I loosen my tie a shade.

Standing here, watching Thatch expressively tell a story to those surrounding him with warm delight upon his face, you would never know he had started to tremble the moment I told him a house full of nosy and meddling people were waiting to harass and interrogate him. Which brought about the tie situation, which I didn't mind at all.

"He looks good," Gowan whispers, standing close to me with Dandy between us. I smile, unable to break my gaze from Thatch laughing at something Quentin said.

"Yeah, he does. Can you believe it?" I ask breathlessly, trying to come to terms with the fact he's here myself. "After the Harvest came and went and he didn't show, I thought … well, I'm just glad he's here now."

Gowan eyes me suspiciously but says nothing, opting to take a drink of her spiced eggnog instead. When she notices me eyeing it, she grins. "Want some? Iris' special recipe."

"Gods, yes."

Was and Wasn't

Thatch

The place I used to sleep no longer exists.

Oh sure the shell of it is here, painted sky blue and blanketed with a crushed carpet that begs you to bury your toes into its softness. Many things rest on the walls, like shelves filled with artifacts and books, but what catches my eye are the seven paintings evenly distributed throughout the room. Beside each one is a gilded frame protecting a sheet of paper filled with handwritten notes. The scrawl is unfamiliar, but each word explains my life in incredibly intimate detail.

The bathroom is still here, but it's no longer used for that purpose. The tub that Arlo and I once bathed in together is gone, the tiled floor we splashed water onto whilst laughing has been ripped up and replaced with wooden planks. The once-bathroom is as warm as the once-bedroom, furnished with a rocking chair and a pull out couch which has a thick flannel blanket laid over its leather arm, both are situated under the window on the end wall. The four-paned rectangle offers a view of the outbuildings I've learned are roosts for the avian familiars. I run my fingers across the flannel and sigh, studying the framed articles on the walls. They're all printed by the same press, The Radickal Magickal Gazette, and they're all about Watchers, about Arlo, about me.

A photograph catches my eye, resting on a small desk beside the rocking chair. It's in black and white, which seems odd considering color photography has been around for quite some time. It's a five by seven, and appears it might've been taken here on the island, if the familiar evergreens composing the background are anything to go by.

In the center stands Arlo and a man who comes up to his chest, a wisp of a thing that makes Arlo look even larger than he already is. He's fairly young, dressed in jeans and a leather jacket like his companion. He's wearing an eye patch, and his ears stick out just a little bit from beneath his hair. His lips are thin and quirked up ever so slightly, like he's reluctantly amused by something Arlo had said. Both have their arms crossed and stand side by side, like perhaps it was supposed to be a serious pose, but the moment captured is something far more beautiful.

Arlo is laughing, full and bright, face upturned to the sun. The man's waist-length, brunet curls are tossed over his shoulder, the one pressed against Arlo's. They're obviously close, but I have no idea who this person is, nor heard Arlo talk about anyone who makes him laugh like that. A bad feeling settles in my gut as I contemplate just how little Arlo has actually told me about the years he was fighting for all of their lives. I've done nothing but cry and sleep, missing the bigger picture.

I pick up the frame, tracing the man's face, then Arlo's. In the bottom right corner is a signature, and it's then I realize it's not a photograph at all, but a pencil drawing. "My stars," I whisper, wondering who crafted such a beautiful piece, who memorized the moment and brought it to life. There's a caption there too, below the signature. *'The Last Laugh.'*

I set down the frame with care, it feels incredibly heavy as I do. I take a seat on the couch and glance around the room again, the haunting feeling I was trying to avoid has magnified by tenfold. For all intents and purposes, both rooms seem to be a small museum of sorts, but they *feel* like a memorial.

I turn my attention to the window, looking past the frosted glass. Evergreens meet my lost gaze, burdened with snow. If I look hard enough, I can see where the forest thins out, near the beach. I can picture Arlo sitting on this couch, curled up beneath that blanket and waiting, waiting, *waiting*.

"I can't tell you how many times I've found Arlo in that exact same spot," Quentin Matsdotter says from behind me, surprising but not startling me. I look over my shoulder, finding him standing in the doorway with his hands in his pockets. He's wearing black slacks and a white button up, the sleeves rolled up to his elbows. His forearms are covered in tattoos now, all books and runes, swords and quills. A glittering gold bow tie finishes the look, which matches his big round glasses.

Pesto runs past him, knocking into his calves before jumping onto the couch. I chuckle, scratching the goat between the ears. "It's a nice place to sit and wait awhile."

Quentin watches me, unsure. "Would you like some company? I'm sure you probably came up here to get away from the noise for a little while, if you'd like I can leave."

I pat the cushion and Pesto *screams*, running out of the room just as quickly as he'd come. I wince, looking at Quentin. "Please, come sit with me. I was merely satisfying my curiosity."

Quentin strides over with purpose, snatching up the blanket before plopping beside me. He tucks his legs beneath him, then covers us both with the blanket. I chuckle, making myself a little more comfortable beside him. "Yes, this is quite nice," I say, grinning at him.

I catalog how he's changed over the years, the past decade has been mostly kind to him and he's developed fine wrinkles. His hair is a little longer than it was before but not much, curling around his ears in a good mix of silver and black. His thick stubble is dark, trimmed artfully. It appears his nose has been broken more than once, there's also a few scars that litter his left cheek. My gaze travels down and I can't help but linger for a moment too long on the thin scar across his throat, it ripples when he swallows. I gaze out the window, then back to his face.

"Arlo tells me you and Loch had quite the run for a while there." I try, then clear my throat. "Well, he really hasn't said much in the way of details, just that you two had the worst of it, and that you saved his life. I wanted to thank you, for taking care of him."

Quentin chuckles, nuzzling the blanket against his flushed cheek. "Ah, yes. You don't need to thank me, I would do it again, he's Arlo, you know? It was ... well, I think our adventures are a story for another time. Nothing compared to what you went through, I'm sure."

I lift a shoulder. "Everyone's struggles are valid, and there is no need to compare the size of them to make it so."

Quentin laughs, and it's warm. "This is true."

We talk for a little while, about small things like Gowan's children, and Kitt and Lindsey's new apartment in *Etz Hayim.* Then the small things snowball into bigger things. He tells me how he hasn't seen Arlo smile like *this* for so long. I tell him that I've never felt more at home, anywhere.

In the distance someone calls, "It's time for dinner!" Even though it's just past two in the afternoon. Quentin stares out the window wistfully, watching Felix and the other young witches throw snowballs at each other. Calen's head pops up from behind a snow wall upon hearing the word *dinner* shouted by someone out of view, then is spectacularly hit in the face with a snowball. He chuckles quietly, soft and lost in thought.

I imagine Arlo sitting there, watching. Waiting.

"Was he alright?"

Quentin turns his attention to me. His eyes aren't the same green as Arlo's, they're brighter and resemble summer grass under a hot sun, but beautiful and captivating in their own right. His jaw ticks while he considers me, and the true answer lies in the seconds it takes for Quentin to put together an acceptable answer.

He tells me the truth, though, and it's as harsh as I expected. Not unkind, but brutally honest.

"He was, and *wasn't*, for a long time. Well, I suspect you know about Leon coming back, if you knew about ... me."

I nod, teeth gritted. Hearing Leon's name stirs a burning anger inside me, but there's nothing I can do to quench it now.

Quentin nods sharply. "That kept his mind off you, but then the first year mark hit, and things were quiet again, for a little while. He got ..." Quentin sighs, pulling the blanket around his chin. "It's not for me to say. You know how he is, big bright smile for everyone else, but when he's alone, well."

"I do. So then ... what, the Hunt came later, right?"

Quentin's lips thin and his nose wrinkles. He glances at the picture on the desk and my heart quickens. "Yes, and then the Hunt came. It was bad, for all of us, but especially him."

"Was he ... alone?"

Quentin blows out a big breath, leaning in towards me. "I mean, we were all there for him, for each other. But as far as, well, someone like *you*, no. There was no one else. That's just Fin." He nods to the picture, like that explains everything.

"I haven't heard about him yet," I admit, and Quentin's eyes widen.

"*Oh*. Oh. Well, I'm sure Arlo will fill you in." He leans back, tugging on a necklace of his. That uneasy feeling festers in my gut and Quentin clears his throat. "But anyway, Levena needed him again, and he answered the call. He always has, always will."

He will always answer the call.

"But not alone." I add, giving him a look. "You were all there for him, and that's the difference."

"I guess so," he says, eyes wandering the room in contemplation before returning back to me. "So ... what about you? Were *you* alright?"

I shrug. "I was, and *wasn't*, for a long time."

"Alright, wiseass," Quentin says, shoving my shoulder.

"Have I lost you before I've had you, love?" Arlo asks, leaning in the doorway with crossed arms and a teasing smirk. I startle, and Quentin *laughs*. Heat warms my neck and I throw the blanket over Quentin's head, rushing to Arlo's side.

I throw my arms around his middle and bury my face into his sternum. I hold him with everything I have, forcing an exhale out of his lungs.

"Oh, what's this for?" Arlo asks, arms rising to encapsulate me. His chin rests in my curls and Quentin's gaze burns into my back, but we are kind of blocking the doorway.

"Nothing, I just missed you."

He chuckles, pressing a kiss to the top of my head. "And I you."

When the three of us make it downstairs, the line of people with empty hands making their way into Big Kitchen and out again in the direction of the 'Main Hall' with full plates collectively turn to *stare* at us. The chatter dies a merciful death, and smiles eerily spread across each face.

I can't help it.

"*What*?" One word slips out with much more stridency and volume than I had intended. Someone laughs in the Den, further breaking the silence.

"Nothing at all," Kitt says, only a few people away from us in line. The smile on her face is *absolutely* sinister. I glance up at Arlo standing close beside me, hand clasping mine.

"Beats me." He shrugs, but the grin on his face is full of mischief and matches Kitt's.

Quentin breaks from us, muttering about Elochian and hiding a snicker behind his hand as he runs away. I roll my eyes, leading Arlo to the back of the line because I *cannot* wait any longer. The scents rolling through Witch House are overwhelming, beckoning me closer and closer.

"You *better* not have anything planned," I mutter, not bothering to look up again because I know my facade of annoyance will falter the moment I see his dumb smile.

"And what makes you think *I* would be the culprit?"

"Because everyone's bad behavior was learned from you."

Kitt and Lindsey laugh, as do some of the young witches standing between them and us. A young lady, Jo, I think? Her cheeks flare pink, eyes bright with curiosity. She whispers to one of Gowan's eldest children standing in the group, which starts a chain reaction of whispers.

Arlo raises a brow, glaring down at the children. They stiffen ramrod straight, cheeks bulging with air as they withhold their gossip. I can't help but laugh a little, especially when Arlo snaps his fingers and pretends to be more interested in the kitchen than the flock of luminescent butterflies taking flight, borne of emerald magick. Somehow, I manage to tear my gaze away from the butterflies dancing on children's wrinkled noses, to Arlo's face.

He's looking at me.

I smile, it's instinct. Reflex. Reaction. *Right*.

He smiles back, and this is it. This day can't possibly get any better.

It does.

And doesn't.

Every person in Witch House waits on lengthy wooden benches, pressed close together with full plates sitting before them on gnarled dining tables. I thought there were a dozen of the elegantly crafted tables, but either I miscounted or more magickally appeared. There are so *many* people gathered, and the space doesn't seem large enough to house them all at first glance, but it *does*. Whether it's a trick of the eye or true magick is involved, the end result is impressive nonetheless. I would dare say there's a hundred people gathered, at least.

No one speaks, and no one eats. At the head of the hall is a massive chalkboard wall, empty and freshly cleaned. Wreaths of firs, pinecones, dried citrus, and flowers of different varieties surround the frame of the chalkboard. Some wreaths have roses, others marigolds and more still have white chrysanthemums. More pinecones lay across the tables, situated haphazardly between candles.

Black, blue, white, and purple tealight candles wait conspicuously in the center of the tables, randomly dispersed and unlit. I fiddle with wax cast in a lavender shade, fighting the urge to dive into my food. Arlo and I had lost each other somehow on the way here, and now I sit between Caspian and Tobias.

I glance at Tobias for answers, but he only gives me a smile. His wings are spelled away and he hasn't aged a day since I saw him last. Perhaps I shouldn't feel this way, but it makes me happy to know I'm not the only one to be mostly unmarked by time. At least, in the natural sense.

The chandeliers hanging in the lofty distance dim slowly, and Arlo appears from seemingly nowhere before the chalkboard wall. Air catches in my lungs and I drop the candle, turning in my seat. I face the head of the hall and lean forward, thigh brushing against Caspian's hip. I briefly lock eyes with him, and he gives me the kindest smile I've ever seen. He takes the candle I had abandoned from the table, then offers it to me.

"You'll want this," He whispers, and I take it with a slow nod.

Caspian glances around, then reaches into his pocket. He offers me a small, velvet satchel with a tag looped through the blue and gold thread cinching the bag closed. I take a closer look at the tag, it simply says *'Arlo.'*

"What's this?"

Caspian puts a finger to his lips, gesturing for me to put it away. "Save it for later. You'll know when you need it."

I nod, sliding the satchel into my pants pocket. I try to puzzle out what he's given me and what it's for. Arlo's name is on the tag so it's obviously intended for him, but why give it to me?

I roll the candle between my fingers again, watching Arlo survey the people gathered together in this sanctuary he's created. My heart swells so much goddamn pride, I very well might cry right here like a fool. A terrible grief entangles with the feeling, soul mourning for every milestone achieved and hardship encountered, all without me.

Arlo paces, hands in his pockets and head down. After a few laps back and forth, he stops at the center of the wall and faces the quiet crowd with a lazy smile. His shoulders roll back and for the briefest of moments his gaze locks onto mine, then he exhales.

"Firstly, I want to welcome you all to another Yule feast, and thank you for bringing enough food to feed an army." Arlo chuckles, raking a hand through his hair. "Each year I'm sure there's no way our festivities can get any bigger, but they do. This year is the largest gathering in Witch House history, and while I know that you all only visit so you don't have to clean up your own homes, it means the world to me, to *us*."

Soft laughter bubbles around me, caressing my anxious spirit. Arlo looks tired, distracted. The flickering connection between us urges me to stand, to go to him.

But what he says next freezes me where I sit.

"We all know how much greater this celebration would be, if we were accompanied by those lost to The Hunt." A shuddering breath courses through Arlo and an orb of emerald light flares in his cupped hands. "While they are not here in body, you can fucking *bet* they're here in spirit. Let us take a moment to acknowledge those who were stolen from us much too soon."

Several things happen at once.

The orb of light dies, revealing a tall, rose shaded candle in his hands.

A tidal wave begins with Arlo at the front of the hall and ends with those standing in rows at the back, magick ignites every wick in rolling succession.

A stick of white chalk rises and sweeps in elegant arcs at the top left corner of the chalkboard wall. Letter by letter, script and mystery unravels, leaving behind a name. *Finnegan Wroughtfern.*

That's just Fin. The Last Laugh.

A second passes before the chalk continues marking down another name.

And another.

And *another.*

Choked whispers and murmurs of '*hello, I miss you, happy Yule, goodbye,*' float through the air, twirling around the candles being released into the atmosphere at different frequencies of grief. Some people say what they need to immediately and gently loft their candle into the air, watching it float away. Others take longer, either they struggle for words or have too much to say.

Tobias and Caspian release their candles wordlessly on either side of me.

I watch *dozens* of candles lift into the air at once, sent by Calen, Felix, Lysander, Silas, and all their friends standing together in the center of the room. They are gathered in a circle, heads bowed, arms around each other's shoulders.

Bob and Ren are seated with Helena and Rhea, each of them send up candles and wipe away tears.

I watch, and watch, and watch.

Arlo stares at the candle in his own hands, shoulders slumped and face hidden by a curtain of hair. I had initially thought that the pale rose candle could be meant for me, but I'm here. A burning sensation creeps down my throat, and I don't like it. I'm not a witch, but I *do* know the symbolism behind the colors. The man, that Fin in the picture ...

Am I overthinking this?

And if I'm right, do I even have a reason to be angry?

Can I *blame* him for being human? For needing someone to love him?

I look down at the burning tealight in my own hands, waiting for release.

I stand.

I go to him.

His head jerks up when I join his side, wax spills onto his palms but he doesn't flinch. Something complicated crosses his face, but the tears trailing down his cheeks are self-explanatory. His eyes are wide and fearful, like he was awoken from a bad dream. A quiet crack runs down the center of my heart, and my soul cries for everything he lost.

I bring the candle in my hands closer to my face. I watch the flame sputter, wick turn black. I inhale, then nearly extinguish it with my exhalation filled with true sorrow. Sorrow for the people who died for senseless reasons, for my not being here. For Arlo, for the person he cries for.

"For all the lives lived, and lost, loved, and stolen. I thank the ones who kept the man beside me alive, and happy, and loved, when I could not do so."

When the last whispered word escapes, my candle lifts as if drawn by a gentle magnet. The flame brightens and I watch it go, so distracted that at first I don't notice Arlo has sent his off too. They spiral lazily around each other, as if the pillar and tealight are dancing together on their ascent.

"Thank you," he says, quiet and broken. Arlo's fingers brush against mine, asking for permission. I immediately take his hand in mine and squeeze tight. I search his red-rimmed eyes and open my mouth to ask if he loved Fin, if that's who he cries for.

"Come here," I whisper, pulling him into me. Arlo hunches over and buries his face in my neck. My arms encircle his shoulders and his tighten around my waist.

"I love you."

"I know, *leva*. I know."

I'm not sure how long we stay that way, it feels like forever, but when Felix gently nudges me, the logical part of my brain supplies that it's only been minutes. Felix stands tall beside us and opens his mouth, but the gentle *clack* of the chalk touching down on the tray running along the bottom of the board interrupts the silence that is overwhelmingly *loud* now.

At last, all the names have been marked.

It's haunting, necessary, and ... stars, *why*?

Wouldn't this tragedy have caught the attention of *the* Gods?

Burn Shit

Arlo

"Why don't you two go sit down, I'll finish," Felix whispers, and his voice is what finally knocks me out of it. I inhale everything that is Thatch one more time, then straighten.

Thatch's striking sky blue eyes are the first thing I see, and they're softened by worry. There is a hardness to his jaw though, it demands questions, and perhaps there's a little anger lingering in the subtle lines wrinkling his brows. Whether it's directed at me or something else I don't know, but it feels right that it would be because of me.

I didn't think … I didn't think this would happen. I thought I had buried my grief.

I blink and we're on the side of the hall, Thatch's hand is tight on mine and he's *still* looking at me. I look around suspiciously, wondering how the fuck we got here so fast. Felix is standing where we were before, picking up where I left off. He gives me a subtle glance and gently probes my mind with a question.

"Do you need to leave?"

"*No.*"

"Are you alright?" Thatch asks, drawing my attention back to him.

"Yes, fine. I tend to get a little emotional during the holidays, I'm sorry."

His eyes track my face, moving back and forth. "Don't apologize, I can only imagine how difficult it is for you." His lips press together and his gaze slides to the board, to the top left corner. "You lost so much, all of you. I had no idea ... the extent of it, I suppose." There's nothing unkind there, perhaps testing.

I stare at the name. "Fin was a writer, all those articles upstairs? They're his. He played a big part in fighting against the AWO and NOJ in ways we couldn't, and in the end, he never got to see it." I inhale sharply, and Thatch's pupils restrict. "It wasn't—"

"Alright, seeing as how this is the part where we *usually* tell stories about a certain mischievous immortal and send up a candle for him, we're going to do something a *little* bit different this year." Felix's booming voice startles Thatch and his attention whips around, finding a room full of people staring at us.

"You—*what*? For me?" Thatch runs a hand through his curls, yanking as he goes. "Wh—"

"Shh, none of that." Kitt chastises, waving him off as she approaches. Her hips sway in the forest green, form fitted dress she wears, tail flicking behind her. In her hands is a good sized box tied up in a bright green bow. She thrusts it into Thatch's arms and he nearly drops it, recovering with an *oof*. I can't help but laugh, and it hurts (heals).

"Why is it so heavy?" He asks, looking between me, her, and everyone else watching with obvious excitement.

"Open it," I say, squeezing his shoulder gently. "We've been waiting a long time for you to open it."

He does without another word, primly untying the ribbon and draping it around his neck so as not to lose it. After a little more fussing, he finds what's inside. His brows pull together as he tries to work out what it is at first, then soften when he cradles the leather bound and bulging book in his shaking hands. He opens it to the first page, and a little gasp escapes him.

I know each entry by heart, but especially the first. I wrote it one week after he left, noting everything that happened in a conversational tone, like he was there with me. The first few are from me, then Caspian discovered what I was doing. The next day he delivered two letters, one from him and one from Tobias. Word spread, and letters began piling up from everyone.

Kitt, Lindsey, Quentin, Elochian, Gowan, even Iris.

Felix.

Silas.

When Calen came and learned about him, they wrote him a letter to him too, full of random thoughts and all about 'her people.'

Everybody had something to say to Thatch, so we bound words and pages into a book just for him. Miles turned out to be a bookbinder of exceptional quality and took care of the finer details, merging years worth of pages into not just one beautiful tome, but three. The one in Thatch's hands is the first, and it's been waiting for this moment for years.

We all have.

Does he *feel* it now, how much everyone loves him?

"I don't know what to say, this is ... oh my stars, thank you." Thatch's voice breaks on sharp tears and he sniffles, tearing his gaze from the pages to everyone who is watching the moment unfold with such fondness. "I needed this."

"There's two more back at your guy's place, but as you said they're a bit *weighty*," Kitt says, an arm slung around Lindsey's shoulders.

Lindsey's ruby red lips pull into a wide smile, her dress matches Kitt's but is a beautiful navy instead of green. She says, "Happy Yuletide, Thatch."

'Happy Yuletide, Thatch, Thatcher, Scarlet,' echoes through the Main Hall.

I keep Thatch's pieces together with an arm around his shoulders. He leans into me and looks up, smiling through the tears. I kiss his forehead, whispering, "Happy Yule, love."

We're swept back into the thick of it, towards plates full of food that are surely cold by now. Thatch and I are separated, Felix somehow got a hold of him and they're both laughing ahead of me, heads bowed and eyes on the book.

I can't help it.

My eyes wander to the name in the upper left corner of the blackboard.

I wanted him to be here for this. I wanted them to meet. I wanted him to *not* die.

Thatch won't stop fucking *moaning,* and I'm pretty sure *I'm* about to perish where sit.

"This is absolutely wonderful, what's it called again? Bread *pudding*? Well, I never." Thatch shovels another bite overflowing with maple syrup into his mouth, and tearing my gaze away from his lips wrapping around the spoon is impossible, that's all there is to it. He's engrossed in conversation with Caspian of all people, both sit across the table from me. I take full advantage to gawk at Thatch's pale throat as it works and the lines crinkling his eyes when he chuckles.

"You're drooling, Da." Serena whispers, subtly nudging my shoulder with her curled horn.

"Am not," I mutter, stabbing into my apple pie with such force the steel plate squeaks. My ears burn and Serena snorts, burying her amusement in a slice of pumpkin. The faun has her nose in everyone's business but not with malicious intent, merely there as a friend and giving a nudge when needed. She spreads good luck magick wherever she goes, and isn't afraid to call people out for being an idiot.

Currently, that idiot is me.

"Dude, you literally have *drool* on your tie."

I look, because of course I do.

"Oh my Gods," I groan at the sight of my loose but clean tie.

Serena is really giggling now, and I retort by elbowing her. That only causes her to laugh harder, throwing her head back and shaking her colorful mohawk. Thatch looks between us quizzically, brow raised. His gaze travels down to my tie, then he rolls his eyes and scoffs. He stands and leans over the table, beckoning me with a come hither motion.

"You're hopeless," Thatch says, nose wrinkling when I don't stand immediately.

I don't make him wait long.

I stand and push my plate back from the edge, leaning across the table filled with food and surrounded by our family. Music softly plays from Calen's enchanted speakers nestled into the distant ceiling, strings and ivory keys wash away the sounds of everyone else but us. He squints a little and his tongue sticks out between his teeth as he readjusts my tie, then smooths out the front of my vest that matches his, but cast in a deep scarlet instead of blue.

"There, that's—"

When Thatch's sky blue attention meets mine, his words die in his throat. I'm not sure what he finds on my face, but it must be good because his fingers slip around my tie and he tugs me gently towards him. My back arches and I'm sure he's on his toes, but we close the distance and our lips meet with the lightest of greetings. His long eyelashes flutter shut, candlelight plays across them and the urge to kiss each lash comes over me. I don't close my eyes, not this time.

Hours, or in all reality, seconds, pass. His eyes open, pupils overtaking his iris upon capturing me in his sight. His lips part into a shy smile and he breathes, leaning back.

I breathe, standing tall as the crimson fabric of my tie slips through his fingers.

And I need him.

Gods, I've never needed him like I need him right *now*.

But that sly fox winks at me, taking a seat between Caspian and Tobias again like nothing happened at all. No one else comments upon the moment either, and I sit in a starstruck daze, bumping into David who shifts into a *malakim* with great sapphire wings.

"*Oof*," David says, shaking out his now long and bright blue hair after his form finalizes.

"Sorry Dave, I didn't mean to jolt you," I say, cheeks aflame.

He smiles wide and instantaneously, wings fluttering and sending feathers aloft. "It's alright Dad, things happen when we get excited, am I right?"

I chuckle at the familiar sentiment that I had passed onto the shapeshifter after our first lessons, shortly after I learned that David might not *ever* be able to control his shifts. Trauma wrecks the body and mind, magick too. "Right, buddy." I ruffle his hair and he preens under my touch, one of the many young ones who love it when I give them even the simplest of attention. With the body of an adult and the mind of someone *much* younger, I don't think he'll ever grow out of it. Serena beams at him, her brother in all but blood.

When I straighten in my seat, Serena gives me an *'I told you so'* look, but says nothing else, smiling nearly as hard as I am. I take a *long* drink of spiced eggnog to drown the giddy sensation, wishing Gowan was here to refill it.

"Say, isn't Yuletide technically *tomorrow*?" Thatch asks between bites.

"Have you two been that busy fornicating that you've told him nothing, Arlo?" Tobias jests, and I suffocate on my last sip of eggnog. Everyone is trying to *choke* me today.

Thatch laughs, long and bright. "I'm afraid I've been stripping the ceiling of it's paint since coming home, that's all."

"Well that explains it," Caspian says, eyes filled with pure evil. I try to stop him with a glare but of course, he keeps right on going.

"Explains what?" Thatch asks over his last bite.

"Why Arlo has been thirsting so hard he's drying out the room. You should've seen him earlier, he—"

I clear my throat and Caspian's scarf encircles his face, blocking his mouth. He yanks it down, laughing.

"Don't listen to him," I say, but the damage is done.

Thatch grins at me, brows raising. "Poor thing."

Sweat dampens my collar and I loosen my tie, immediately earning a fierce look of irritation and desire. "*Techincally*, the solstice *is* tomorrow, but everyone will want to be home and not traveling. It's easier to do all this," I gesture vaguely around the room. "On the day before. Everyone gets sent home with food too, so they don't have to cook the next day."

Caspian grumbles, and I roll my eyes. "Unless you're Cas and insist on doing everything yourself, they have two big feasts, two days in a row."

"I'm certainly not complaining," Tobias says, rubbing his stomach.

Caspian smiles at Tobias, eyes glittering.

To keep myself busy, I take one of the pinecones littered across the table, then withdraw a pen and notepad from inside my vest. Thatch curiously watches me jot down a few things on a piece of paper, then tear it from the pad and fold it down. He finally leaves his fork behind when I tuck the paper inside a crevice of the pinecone.

"What're you doing?" Thatch asks, pie crust crumbs lingering on the corner of his lips.

"Making a wish." I chuckle, reaching forward to wipe off the remainders of his dessert with my thumb. He blushes, wiping at his mouth for good measure. "You write down your wishes for the next year, then later we'll burn them. Here, we can share one."

"Oh," Thatch says, taking the materials I've offered. "Like ... anything?"

I shrug. "Why not?"

Thatch immediately sets to work, tongue poking out and nose scrunching as he writes furiously. Serena pats my shoulder upon standing. "I'm going to find Jamie, it's about time, isn't it?"

"Yeah, a few more minutes." I nod, looking around for Felix. I spy him talking to the fire witch in question across the room, and I smile a little. I've had to do less and less over the years in terms of party organizing, and I'll be forever grateful for Felix.

My smile fades a little and I drop my stare at my hands. "Looks like they're over with Felix and the others."

Serena nods, then looks around me to get David's attention. "Wanna come with me?"

David practically flies out of his chair, shifting into a female *katan* with a mohawk that matches Serena's before he touches the ground. "Yeah, yup. Let's go."

I smile quietly watching them go, and when I turn my attention back to the table Thatch is watching me with something like warm pride. I readjust my rolled up sleeves, head ducked. "What?"

Thatch laughs, surprising me. "Nothing, nothing at all."

"Alright everybody, you know what time it is!" Calen shouts from the head of the hall, waving wildly with Felix and the others at their side. "Let's go burn shit!"

Felix snickers, leaning over to whisper something into Calen's ear,

"Wood, I mean. Sorry, let's go burn some wood!"

Confession

Thatch

I paid no attention to the firepit when Arlo and I had re-united in the backyard of Witch House days ago, but I most certainly would've remembered if it was *this* big.

Right?

"Do you witches ever *not* use your magick?" I grumble, arms crossed and teeth chattering a little bit.

Dinner didn't start until closer to three than two, and now dusk veils the world. In the spaces that light remains, snow falls in heavy waves and threatens to dim the land completely. The powder on tree limbs from the previous night has been added to, weighing down the branches until some dare to scrape the snow banks surrounding the trunks. Thankfully there's no wind, otherwise I'd be completely frozen.

"Sometimes." Arlo chuckles, sliding an arm around my shoulders. He pulls me into his side, and I immediately melt into him. "But you'll find that magick is in never ending supply around here. Have you got the pinecone?"

I reach into my vest pocket, ensuring that it is indeed tucked away. "Sure do."

A pale skinned and black haired human approaches us, warily glancing at me although it's clear their intent is to speak with Arlo. "Hey, Ba. Any special requests this year?"

Arlo shrugs, holding me even closer to him, so much so that it's a little hard to breathe. "You're the master at work here Jamie, you do you. Thatcher, this is Jamie, our resident fire witch."

I extend my hand to Jamie who stares at it for a moment, then takes it. Their hand is impossibly cold and small, their grip loose. Jamie stares me in the eyes like I've personally wronged them, then leaves without another word.

I glance up at Arlo. "Did I ... do something wrong?"

"No," He brushes a curl away from my eyes, raining snowflakes onto my cheeks. Arlo glances around, we're somewhat isolated from the rest of the crowd surrounding the enormous fire pit. He lowers his lips to my ear, breaking the world with a low tone. "You're ... not the first Watcher that Jamie has met, and their past experience didn't ... it didn't over so well."

"Wh-What? You didn't tell me that—"

Arlo straightens and presses a finger to my lips, eyes brimming with hurt that belongs in my heart. "Later, I *promise*. I wanted to wait until you were ready, but it's not ... not a good story, Thatcher. I didn't think it would ... come up."

I swallow pain and thick emotion, staring up at him like I can find the truth in the subtle wrinkles along his eyes or in the scars peppering his skin. "You *know* how long I've been alone for." I grit out, although I didn't mean to say anything at all.

If I had punched him, the effect would've been lesser than what my words did to him.

He lowers his head. "I–I know."

I sigh, equally pissed off and shamed. "I'm not saying that I'm alone *now*, but ... you know what I mean. I thought I was the last."

"You are, now, as far I know," he says, finally raising his head. "I told you, it's *not* a good story."

"Okay," I say, breathing heavily. "Okay. I believe you, but I still want to know."

"I know." Arlo nods, then faces the fire pit with his hands buried deep in his pockets. I stand by his side, not missing how his eyes glaze over despite the whooping and hollering going on from the rambunctious crowd. My heart thrums with longing, rising anger, and questions.

So many questions.

There's so *much* he hasn't told me.

Jamie stands on the other side of the stone-walled ring, flanked by Calen and a few of their witches that I don't know as well. A tent of dead limbs rises from the concave pit, despite the area being several feet deep the wood stretches high above all of us, even Lysander who is the tallest in the gathering. Jamie frowns at the tented wood, arms crossed and brow pinched. Calen gently hooks their arm through Jamie's, whispering something meant for only the two of them.

Jamie sighs so deeply I can see their chest rising and falling with the effort all the way over here. Jamie nods, rubbing their temple against Calen's before straightening their shoulders. When Calen tries to withdraw, one of Jamie's hands clasps over Calen's arm. Calen doesn't appear surprised, only smiles at Jamie until the witch is assured they won't go anywhere.

"Calen is their mother, father, brother, sister. Calen is everything to all of their witches."

I look up to Arlo, finding him watching the same scene as I. "Most call you Dad, one way or another, and besides Jamie, every one of them have sought you out today with great affection. Miles especially seems to care for you, I saw the two of you talking earlier, and you could see how at peace you make him. All of them, really."

Arlo shakes his head. "It's not the same, and that's fine, that's not what I'm—if it weren't for Calen, none of them would've survived. I know Cae seems ... *bright*, and can be much at times, but Calen is ...."

Arlo trails off when the fingertips of Jamie's free hand alight, acting as wicks for small candle-like flames. The gathering around us increases in volume and density, people collectively stand together and back up a few paces, forming a circular wall around the pit. Whether it occurs naturally or a witch is at work, a sense of belonging and peace ruminates all around me. I stow away my questions and wrap my arm around Arlo's waist, sliding my shoulders under his arm which instantly pulls me tight to his side once more.

I lift on my toes and his shoulder dips without question, his golden eyes are set on the flames stretching above us like scarves in the wind. I bring my lips to his ear, breathing faster than I should be. "Do you know what my last thought was, before the second time we met?" I ask none too softly, but compared to the excitement roaring around us, my words are a murmur.

He looks at me then, a subtlety of eyes shifting and lips quirking. "What's that?"

I roll my bottom lip between my teeth for a hesitant moment before answering. "I thought, *Sparks are flaring, is that fire?*"

Twin suns that can't decide if they want to be emerald or gold drop to my parted lips, setting me aflame.

"And then, I crashed into you."

Arlo Rook laughs then, a sound so raucous and carefree that it splits me right down the middle. Dead wood catches like a spark to the finest tinder as he throws his head back, soulmark a beacon in the night. Flames explode high into the sky in a cacophony of colors that represent every single witch standing around it. Familiars howl, cry, hoot and call into the night. Over the roarous noise of such combined power, is the Hedge Witch who brought them all together.

Laughing, and *laughing*.

Despite the fact I have no idea what he's laughing at, I can't help but giggle. Not laugh, but truly giggle because he's so damn *giddy*. "What's so funny?" I manage, a free hand pressed to my full stomach.

Arlo wipes a tear from his eye with the back of his hand, then pulls me to his front in a slow and easy movement. One hand encompasses the small of my back, while the other finds the curls overhanging my eyes, twisting bright red around dark fingers. My cheeks flush with the eyes pressing into my back, but I ignore them.

I ignore them, because he's looking at me like I'm the only person who exists.

Like I exist.

"I have a confession to make, my love."

My heart speeds with excitement, not fear. "Oh?"

Arlo smiles nervously, a warm hand cupping my snow dusted cheek. His breathing is incredibly fast, pupils restricted and tongue continually darting out to lick his bottom lip as he struggles through words. I open my mouth to ask what's wrong but *instead*, he changes everything.

"I did it on purpose."

I blink rapidly. Snow falls in another heavy sheet. "What?"

"I saw you coming a mile away, and not because of this gorgeous hair." He leans down, pressing a kiss to my forehead blanketed in said curls. "You were laughing, over all the noise, all the chaos, that was the only thing I heard. You were standing in a Soul Mirror booth, and you were laughing. It was this sound that I had never heard in my entire life, but felt more *right* than anything else I've encountered. You went booth to booth, not to buy anything, but to talk with the people, and you were just—"

Arlo huffs out a laugh, combing a shaking hand through his snowflake filled hair. There's *hundreds,* and his hair is so wonderfully long now. "I couldn't gather the courage to actually *speak* with you, so when you were just *standing* there in the middle of the street, watching them prepare the fireworks with that wild look in your eyes, I ... sort of accidentally-purposely walked into you."

I gape at him.

"You growled at me for not watching where *I* was going!"

"Well I had to make it believable, didn't I?"

And then, I laugh too.

The ground shakes with it. The fire jumps in height. Every set of eyes that wasn't on us before watches us with intent now, but I don't care.

"You remembered me. One way or another, you remembered me." I manage between guffaws that pain my abdominals with such aching exquisiteness.

Arlo kisses me, swallowing my laughter whole.

He grounds me to this world with nothing but his body and soul, and the planet continues turning like it always has.

It's some time later that the children come for Arlo.

Long benches that are much more rugged than the ones inside have been pulled around the fire which burns steadily. Cups of spiced eggnog, whiskey, and cider have found their way into the hands of adults who occupy most of the benches. Children, both those who live here and those who don't, run around the backyard and chase each other with snowballs. How they have so much energy, I'll never know. Arlo is seated on a bench with Felix, Lysander, Kitt, and Lindsey. I stand behind Arlo, hands on his shoulders. I occasionally steal a sip of his eggnog, which is *superb*. Our wishes have long since turned to smoke, and many other people have tossed their pinecones into the fire as well.

Silas, Calen, and a few others have disappeared inside, but Arlo assures me it's only temporary. Nonetheless, the gathering is in full swing and I indulge in people-watching with a small smile that won't go away. A few people, Quentin included, are set up with big lap drums and a metallic instrument I've not seen before, something called a hang drum which has a much brighter and haunting sound than it's companions. Arlo is in a full debate with Kitt about something that I had stopped paying attention to some time ago, which is why I notice the incoming wave first.

"Um, Arlo?" I say, squeezing his shoulder.

"Hm? *Oh*, boy. Felix, you ready?" Arlo reaches across Lysander to shove at a cozy Felix all curled into the fae's side. Oliver yelps from beneath Lysander's feet and takes off running, not waiting for his witch to follow. The swamp witch rolls his eyes, giving me a knowing look like I'm in on the secret that is Felix and Arlo's shenanigans.

"Huh, what? Oh, *shit*." Felix scrambles upwards, yanking Arlo with him. The pair take off running towards the woodline, jumping over snow banks, tripping and falling as they go. The dozens of kids that *had* been coming this way veer off towards them immediately, squealing and screeching as they run.

"What in the world?" I murmur, watching the fiasco.

"Just another Yuletide tradition." Lysander pats the now empty space beside him and I have no choice but to take it. "They'll be back."

I fiddle with the hem of Arlo's (my) jacket that he had fetched for me earlier, unsure what to say. "I've never really celebrated before, but I don't think grown men being chased by children has ever been part of the itinerary."

Lysander chuckles. "Yeah, well. They're in charge of String Tree, so when the kids get sick of waiting for their presents, they tend to torture Arlo and Felix for information. It's kind of a running bet every year to see how long it'll take, they actually waited a lot longer than last time."

I laugh, shaking my head. "That's wonderful. Never a dull moment here, I imagine."

"You can say that again."

"Do you like it here?" I ask, surprising Lysander and myself with the bluntness of it.

"Of course, I ..." Lysander looks down at his wringing hands, his lengthy bleach blond hair and the leaf fronds sprouting from his crown tickle his lap. "I lived for so long by myself, and I find it hard sometimes without that solitude."

I reach over and take his hand, lightly. He doesn't pull away, and when my thumb brushes over a patch of moss on the back of his knuckles, he sighs. Lysander's eyes meet mine, and I smile at him. "I know the feeling, and there's nothing wrong with that. Thankfully, we have some pretty understanding people in our life."

Lysander smiles back, just a little. He glances around, then leans in closer to me. "I can't believe it sometimes, that this is ... my *family*, you know? Like in a good way."

"Oh, I know."

"Excuse me, Thatcher?"

I look up, and up. Miles stands a few feet away from us, hands twitching at his sides.

I stand and offer my hand to him, giving what I hope is a warm smile. "Oh, hello. Miles, right? I know we haven't officially met yet, but I've heard from Arlo about you."

"Yes, that's me." Miles shakes my hand, thankfully his grip is relatively firm but not bone crushing. "I was wondering if we could talk for a minute."

"Oh," I say, shifting on my feet. I look back to Lysander, or the place where he once was. "Sure, right here?"

Miles shakes his head. "Maybe somewhere a little bit quieter?"

"Oh," I say again, unsure what he could want to talk to me about. "Lead the way."

Miles leads me away from the fire and around the side of the house. He sighs, then steels himself. "Do you know ... has Arlo told you what my specialty is?"

I blink rapidly. "Oh, um, no he hasn't. Just that you came with Calen a few years ago, and you're very kind and helpful around Witch House. I also understand you bound those gorgeous books for me, so thank you for that."

The orc's pale green skin flushes at that, and I smile a little despite the fact I'm equal parts worried and curious. "Oh. Well. That's—I try my best. But, oh, my specialty. Threads."

"Threads?"

"Yes. I can see threads. Life threads, magick threads. Soul-mate threads especially, they're the brightest. I don't know what they're all actually called, that's just what I call them."

"Oh, stars." I swallow. I know exactly what he's talking about. "That's quite a powerful one, is it not?"

"Yes, it is." Miles sighs again, rubbing a hand over his smooth head. When he speaks again, his throat clogs with emotion. "I wanted to ask you a favor. I don't even know if you can do it, but I thought if anyone could, then it would be you. I was going to wait, I know you probably have so much going on, but I—"

"What is it?" I ask, heart pounding in anticipation. I take a step towards him.

"Can you ... make it stop? I don't want to see them anymore."

I take a step *back* and stare at the witch, this rare and powerful witch that is asking me with tears in his eyes to take away his *magick*. Something so integral and *him*.

"Thatcher?" Miles asks, and I realize I haven't spoken in some time.

"I don't ... I don't understand. You don't ... want to be a witch anymore? Is that what you're saying?"

Miles exhales, a violent and shuddering thing. "I don't want to see the threads anymore. If ... if taking my magick is the cost, then so be it." His eyes slide shut and his head bows. "You have no idea how difficult it is to walk through spiderwebs. For people to constantly be asking me who their people are, and how *angry* they are when I prove them wrong. I just want to live peacefully. I never wanted this."

I regain ground. I take Miles' face in my hands. His eyes shutter open, pupils widening.

"I don't think I can do that, Miles."

"Can't, or won't?" He asks, nostrils flaring.

I give him a sad smile. "Do you know how incredibly rare you are?"

Miles shakes his head, but not roughly. "I don't care. Please, if there's even a *chance*." Miles drops to his *knees,* arms going around my waist like a child, and he cries. "*Please*, help me."

My hands hover above his shoulders and air passes through my lungs in short bursts, oh how I wish Arlo was here to tell me what to do. My heart and head are telling me two different things, and as of right now my heart is pressed to the orc's wet cheek.

I inhale deeply.

Rest my hands on his shoulder and the back of his head.

Close my eyes.

I search through the fabric of this finely woven world, one I crafted together so long ago. It's not hard to find him. Miles is there, his witch's heart and soul pumping a mournful blue into the universe. With tender care, I take his thread into my ghostly hands. Somewhere in the distance, two bodies gasp sharply, one on their knees and the other standing tall.

I call the magick giving fibers interwoven into a person's soul witch threads, but I'm quite sure that's not the technical term. Witch threads are composed of *thousands* of minute filaments that provide different aspects of power, but only a select few determine a witch's specialty. Attempting to split hairs and mute the correct nerves so to speak, is near impossible.

But I have to try.

It's not the first time I've circumvented the universe's will.

Time passes.

Snow collects on my shoulders.

Birds sing into the fleeting sun.

I breathe, exhaling, "Miles."

He asks, "Did it work? Thatcher, did it work? I'm scared."

"Don't be scared. Here." I help Miles to his feet, his knees shake and his eyes are firmly shut.

"It's ... quieter. But I don't feel any different."

"I suppose you'll have to open your eyes then, and see."

Miles blinks open his eyes, very slowly. I'm the first thing he focuses on, and he says, "*Oh.*"

And, "How?"

And, "There's nothing coming out of your body. You're ... normal."

And with great trepidation and tears in his eyes, "Am I still a witch?"

I rest my hands on his shoulders, and my fingers might be shaking a little from the miracle I've performed here today. I don't tell Miles that the laws have been bent in his favor, but the little gasp that escapes between his tusks when I say, "*Yes,*" tells me he already knows.

He picks me up then, hands swooping under my armpits and cheek rubbing against my curls. A rush of air escapes me, and I hug him back. "Thank you, thank you. My Gods, *thank* you."

"It's okay, it's okay."

Everything is okay.

After a few minutes, Miles gently sets me back down on the earth. He shyly smiles at me, then looks back over his shoulder to the house. New instruments have filled the air with their laughter and it's so beautiful that my heart aches with it. "We're going to miss it if we don't go back."

"Oh? Well, we can't have that." I nod and give him a small smile, exhaustion settling fully into my bones. We walk side by side, and he glances at me a few times. Eventually I have to ask, "What?"

"It's just ... even after I told you what I was, you didn't ask."

"Ask what?"

He chuckles, coming to a stop at the corner of the house. Most of the crowd around the fire pit has moved to a different section of the backyard, surrounding a tall pole with strings stretched out in every direction from the top. The strings descend into the woodline, destinations unknown. The musicians are blocked from view, but glimpses of them can be seen every now and then between the loosely packed bodies. Arlo is plain to see, an arm slung around Kitt's shoulders as the *qieren* tells a story, her tail flicking back and forth. He only has eyes for her, and his smile is so warm it burns me even at this distance.

"Exactly."

I look up to Miles, who is watching me.

"I considered it. But you said everyone asks you for proof, and I'm not everyone." I turn my attention back to Arlo, just as he shoves a handful of snow down the back of Kitt's knee-length puffer jacket. I chuckle at the following battle that commences between them. "I have all the proof I need."

When Witches Sing

Arlo

Squeals, grumbles, and hurried conversation ensues. The worn out but no less excited children wait with a hand on the String Tree. Cantrips of light float lowly in the hazy atmosphere, ready to accompany those exploring the woods. Silas and Lysander stand off to the side, sharing a look that is the definition of uneasy. Calen plays their violin, a familiar instrument that doesn't hurt my heart anymore. Unable to stop now that they've begun, Calen dances on the outskirts of our group, accompanied by a few other musicians.

"Is that … ?" Thatch asks, trailing off as we watch Calen dance like they've known nothing else. I kiss his forehead, inhaling crisp winter and cedar. Dewdrop flies overhead from one tree to another, chirruping as she goes.

"Yes. I gave it to Cae last year, for their birthday."

"Oh, good." Thatch murmurs, arms tightening around my waist. "What's wrong with Lysander and Silas?" He asks, rosy cheeked. There's a bruising under his eyes that wasn't there before, and he's holding onto me like I'm everything.

"They aren't a fan of surprises to say the least, but Lysander especially." Felix remarks with a smug grin, standing at my other side. He rocks back and forth on his heels, winking at Lysander when the fae glances over at us. Lysander only glares at Felix, and I snicker.

"Go on, quit teasing him," I say, and Felix practically runs to the String Tree, followed by Oliver.

Thatch pulls away from my side and cocks his head, watching the theatrics unfold. His hand takes a tight hold of mine, and I squeeze. "Surprises?"

"Watch."

Out of the corner of my eye, I notice Caspian elbowing Thatch who looks back at him, bewildered. Then Cas makes a face, and Thatch's lips form a silent *oh*.

"Alright, on your mark," Felix shouts over the giddy excitement from kids and adults alike, because even though the grown-ups don't participate in the scavenger hunt, we still exchange gifts and love to watch the spectacle.

"Get set," Felix has to yell louder this time, Calen's music reaches a crescendo. Dusan's brought several of the kids from the Castle like she does every year, and I'm pleased to see some of the teenagers from there have joined up with the ones from here.

"Go!" Music crashes. Young and old pursue their strings into the unknown in search of magick. It makes me happy to see those reclaiming their childhood, even in a small way, even if only for a moment. Dozens of light cantrips fan out, following hurried footsteps into the evening.

"*Oh*," Thatch says aloud this time, eyes wide. He's looking up at me with a strange look on his face. "The presents are at the end of the strings, aren't they?"

I chuckle. "Yes. Felix's idea, we've been doing it for a few years now."

"But, how did you do it so fast? This wasn't set up here earlier, we walked right by it!"

I press a kiss to the wrinkle in his brow. "*Magick*."

Thatch shakes his head, chuckling. "Just when I think you can't surprise me anymore than you already have."

"If there's anything I can promise you, it's that I will *always* surprise you."

A lazy, full smile takes hold of him. Fire licks my veins. "I'll hold you to that."

He laughs, shaking his head once more. Thatch looks around, and when he notices the many gift exchanges going on around us, he gasps. "Oh Arlo, I didn't know."

"Hey, that's alright. We don't get presents for each person, there's too many of us to do that. Everybody draws a name, some keep it secret, but others know who got them. Like Lysander over there, he knows that Felix got him, but Felix is being a little shit about it and won't tell him what his gift is."

Thatch stares up at me. "That sounds really nice. I've never, um ... heard of something like that before. And you? Who did you have?"

"Well, I actually might have cheated a little." I rub the back of my neck, then reach into my vest with a wavering voice. "There's no rule saying I *can't* buy for more than one person, and I've already given Lindsey her gift. Enchanted ear plugs, Kitt's snoring has gotten *much* worse over the years."

Thatch tracks the movement, pupils widening when he spies the box in my hand. "Don't say that's for me."

"It *is*."

"When the hell did you have time to—oh Arlo." Thatch's shoulders rise and he rolls his bottom lip between his teeth. I wait for him to come to terms with it, and he does so eventually. "Alright, *well*. I have something for you, too." Thatch pushes his words through gritted teeth.

I raise a brow, interest piqued and laughter barely restrained. "Is that so?"

"*Yes*," Thatch snaps, cheeks bright red. He stands before me, this wonderfully handsome man that is all mine. He reaches into his pants pocket, removing a velvet satchel. "On three, we switch."

I want to laugh so bad right now, he's adorably flustered and determined. Tobias doesn't hold back, and Caspian watches us with a wide smile. Kitt and Lindsey have joined our group, chatting dramatically with Serena and David, Gowan and Iris. All of them watch our exchange with pure joy on their faces.

Despite the crowd, Thatch stands resolutely.

"Okay."

"One." His hands creep towards mine.

"Two." My fingers brush against his.

"Three." He gently deposits the bag into my left hand, taking the box I offer in my right. Thatch eyes me suspiciously, holding the box close to his chest. "Open yours first."

"Okay," I say easily, untying the satchel with tortuous movements.

"Hurry up!" Serena says, clapping me on the back. Ramsis flutters in from the snowy atmosphere filled with laughter and gift giving. He lands upon Serena's shoulder, the glitter freckles splattered across his cheeks are quite literally shining.

"Ooh, who had you this year, Dad?" Ramsis asks.

"Dear Thatcher here, apparently," I say, nodding to him.

Thatch blushes and ducks his head, looking down at the box in his hands. When he does, I glance at Caspian. I know his writing better than my own, and if he was trying to be discreet, then perhaps removing the tag would've been a good idea. He raises a daring brow, the numerous lines worn by parenting, near dying, and life I suppose, turn upwards at his eyes and mouth. He says, *'Well, go on then,'* all without actually saying anything aloud.

I give the pixie a look. "Who'd you have?"

He grins, all fangs. "Miles! Can you believe it? I already gave him his gift, some of that weird roquefort cheese of Ren and Bob's, but he liked it just like Felix said he would. Eugenia had me, the little shit. Guess what she gave me?"

I smile, knowing damn well what she got, because Ramsis hates everything but strawberry flavored lip gloss. It's a well known fact. He has a fucking horde that rival's Dusan's gemstone collection, which is saying something.

"Wh—"

"*Aetherberry* gloss, the nerve of that girl!" Ramsis crosses his arms, donning a white turtleneck with golden accents.

"It looks rather handsome on you," Thatch says quietly, drawing everyone's attention. "What? That's what you're wearing now, um, Ramsis, is it?"

Ramsis flushes, tentatively pressing a hand to his lips. "Well of course it does, and ... yes. It's nice to finally meet you, in person."

Thatch smiles, then looks at me. "Well, better get on with it then."

"Alright, alright." I open the bag and peer inside, heart stopping upon seeing the glint of something silver. No, no — *No*, surely this can't be the same ....

I withdraw the pendant by its chain, slowly unveiling its weighted beauty.

A palm sized locket in the shape of a compass, adorned with script initials for the cardinal points. The last time I saw this, it was fractured into at least a hundred pieces, shattered beyond all recognition by a death curse that by all rights should've killed me.

But the locket deflected the curse, and someone else paid the price.

I inhale sharply.

Dewdrop calls, an echoing and low cry from a nearby tree.

I *know* that it's the same pendant I wore for decades and not a replica, even without the familiar energy emanating from its heated surface. There is a spider webbing of cracks composing the compass. I stare at the contrasting metal filling up the fractures, a puzzle cast in silver and gold. Years. Years and years, and my heart is *breaking*.

"It doesn't open anymore," Caspian says quietly. My head jerks up, and I focus on him at Thatch's side. Thatch's bottom lip trembles, and Caspian smiles softly. "Don't be pissed, but ... it's been together for a few years now. I've wanted to give it to you so many times Lo, but I thought—I thought it shouldn't come from me."

"How?" I ask, barely above a whisper. "It was ... the pieces, they were everywhere, the *pieces* were in his *blood* Cas, it wasn't even safe—"

Caspian puts up a hand. "Let's not go there, alright? Just—" He gestures to Thatch who is trying with all his might not to cry. "Put it on already."

We have a bit more of an audience now. Felix and his partners, the rest of the Misfits too.

Thatch gingerly takes the locket from me, stealing some of the frenzied magick buzzing around my fingertips. Our eyes meet and he gives me the softest smile. He kisses my forehead, a barely there touch as if anything more might break me. He reaches around my throat and I shudder, closing my eyes. There's so much I don't want to see there, in the darkness.

I know he's done when the solid weight hangs off my neck, anchoring me.

I breathe.

I open my eyes.

He's there, my person, waiting for me with a warm smile. "Thank you," I say, or try to, but such simple words are overwhelmed by such a simple thing like grief. I want to explain, to tell him that I'm not selfish, and that I'm so glad that he's here.

But that there's a part of me that misses Fin with a goddamn *passion*.

Thatch shakes his head, lips parting, but the glare Caspian bores into him is enough to redirect whatever he was going to say. "You're welcome," Thatch settles on, chuckling a little bit.

"Here, your turn," Tobias says, offering Thatch his forgotten gift. It feels so simple now, and while I know Thatch didn't have anything to do with fixing the locket, but *still* ....

"It's like watching the sweetest, most disgusting holiday movie ever." Elochian mutters from nearby, and I laugh even though it hurts.

Thatch removes the lid from the box, brows furrowed in confusion as he looks inside. "It's ..." He removes a bland sticky note that I found last minute in my office, folded in on itself numerous times.

"A piece of paper?" Serena asks incredulously, but I don't bother to answer her.

Thatch smiles wide, trying to hide his excitement but failing spectacularly. He begins to unfold it, carefully and methodically. Snow crunches as people shift closer, watching eagerly. I've long gotten used to there being hardly any boundaries in this house, but I'm not sure Thatch enjoys being gawked at.

He doesn't make any indication that he's even noticed, instead he unfolds it for the last time. A green dot sits in the center of the paper, and Thatch looks up to me upon finding it. "You've gotten lax," he says, a teasing lilt to his lips.

I shrug. "I didn't want to make you work too hard for it. Go on." I gesture to the paper, not missing the twinkle in his eye upon hearing my words.

Thatch taps the dot once, and nothing happens.

He glances up to me, and I grin. "What was that about being easy?"

"Oh my Gods," Kitty mutters, a hand muffling her sentiment.

"Hm," Thatch says, ignoring the jeers. "What about ..." He trails off, humming to himself. The green dot brightens to white, and he giggles. "Oh! I've got it."

Like it's *nothing*, Thatch sings.

It's familiar, a classic yuletide song that originated centuries ago and is a staple at every holiday gathering. I can't help but wonder if he coined it, but that would be silly.

Right?

The glowing dot expands, heatlessly burning up the page until there's nothing left but sparks of floating white that dance between Thatch and I. He doesn't stop singing.

And I start.

It's an unfamiliar thing, something I've tried over the years since Thatch left, but it never felt right. I've never been much of a singer to begin with, but harmony officially left the building when I was alone (surrounded by people) and going through the motions.

Thatch startles, but he doesn't lose his place in the song. His voice is much lighter than mine, a smooth thing created just for this purpose. I'm rougher, more of a rumble than anything, but the smile that overtakes his face tells me I'm doing something right. I'd sing for an eternity if it meant he would smile like this forever.

When witches sing, the sound is haunting.

Beautiful.

Magickal.

Home.

Felix is the first to join our duet, then Calen.

Tobias and Caspian, the perfect baritone and tenor duo, each a compliment of the other.

Lysander and Silas hum.

Elochian sings, holding Quentin close to his side.

Kitty and Lindsey sing, and kiss, and sing.

Gowan and Iris sway in time to the music.

Doc and Ilisia croon for each other and no one else.

Miles, Serena, and all the other young witches lend their voices to the harmony.

Dusan, and Kleo, and our *family*.

I sing, and Thatch sings with me. His lashes are slightly wet, but he's smiling. The white sparks that had floated high above us once before settle back down into his cupped hands, flaring one final time. A candle rises from the light, a cream colored pillar that smells like the forest surrounding us.

Everyone else keeps singing, but his voice dies. I rest my forehead on his. "It's a Neverlight, the candle's magick. It never goes out, nor does the fire spread. I thought it would be nice, for night time, you know? I'm sorry it's not—"

"No," Thatch says, cutting my whisper off with a tender kiss. "It's perfect, thank you, *leva*."

I grin against his lips. "Yeah?"

"*Yes*," He teases, then his eyes dart to the side. "Everyone is watching us."

"Indeed they are. Want to cause some trouble?"

"Of course," he says immediately, much to my surprise. I give him a devilish smile, reaching inside my vest. I glance around, catching Tobias watching us with a knowing quirk to his lips. I take Thatch's hand, slipping an oval amethyst into it.

Thatch's eyes widen and his fingers shake. He stares at the stone in his palm, lips trembling. "Same words?" He asks, and I remember a day filled with ghosts.

"No, it's only *shemesh* now," I say quietly, and he looks up from the stone immediately.

"Sun?"

I enclose his fingers around the stone, then kiss his knuckles. "My sun."

I don't register his next words. I don't register the rush of wind and magick.

There's only him.

The moment we touch down at home, in our bedroom, Thatch kisses me. He holds me, kisses me, swallows me whole.

"Arlo, please."

"Yes, Thatch, *Yes*."

My waistcoat is peeled off first, then his. My fingers trip over the clips to his suspenders, his over my buttons. Every slide of fabric is torture, and there's no relief until his cool skin presses against mine. My knees hit the back of our bed, the blankets are rumpled from our restless night and I don't mind because that means he is *here*, with me, now.

Thatch straddles my waist, holding my face in his hands like I'm the most precious thing in the world. At that moment,

I would believe him if he said so. I run my thumb over his soulmark, sighing in relief upon seeing it glow for me.

"I love you, do you know that I love you?" He asks between kisses, dragging his lips from my mouth to my adam's apple, then down my chest as he pushes me back, *back*. I gasp, hips bucking when he drags his tongue across a nipple.

"Yes, oh Gods, *please*, show me."

And he does.

The fingers of his right hand create divots in my thick hips. His lips encircle my cock. His left hand slides down the junction of my thigh and pelvis, fingers brushing the underside of my tightened balls. Thatch moans as he takes me in, slow and steady and his tongue is so *hot*.

"*Ah*, fuck." I groan, fisting the blankets at my sides. "Oh, Thatcher, I've fucking missed you."

Thatch hums, tongue flicking over the flushed head of my cock. I jolt when he tugs on my sack, accidentally thrusting forward and riding his tongue. He doesn't gag, in fact he takes me deeper and *fuck*. "I'm going to come," I warn, and he pushes me back. I can't stop my whine of disappointment, but it transforms into a yelp when I'm promptly flipped onto my stomach.

There's so much skin. His cold front, my warm back. Long lines pressed together, entwining and arching and *needing*. His lips are against my ear, air panting through my curls in short bursts. His erection slides against my ass insistently, and a little gasp escapes me. Thatch says, "I want to fuck you, *leva*. You offered that to me once, do you remember?"

"Yes, I remember. I remember everything." I nod quickly, rolling my hips because I need *something*. He moans into the space behind my ear and I shudder as magick rolls throughout my body like a tidal wave. "Fuck me, Thatch. Please."

"Oh Arlo," he says, entire body shaking with those two words. Thatch gently sweeps aside my hair, then leaves kisses across my shoulders, down my spine. His hands explore where his lips do not, and it takes everything in me to remain still under his ministrations. Mostly still, that is.

When he presses an especially tender kiss to the base of my spine, I jolt again.

"So sensitive," Thatch laughs, hands sliding over my hips. He hikes my ass up and my cheek rests against the corner of a pillow, heated from his teasing and my position.

"It's only been a decade or so," I tease, and his fingers stop their trailing over my ass. I look back, meeting his eyes immediately.

"You really waited?" Thatch asks, and it's so incredibly small that my heart cracks like wafer thin glass.

I push myself up until my back has met his front again. I reach behind me and pull his face close, capturing his lips with mine. He kisses me back, but it's unsure now. When his eyes open and our lips part, I say, "There's never been anyone for me but you, Thatcher. I promise."

And he says, "Okay."

He gently folds me forward again.

His hands rest on my ass, spreading me for his tongue which is everything I've fucking needed. An undignified cry escapes into the blankets, and Thatch's amusement hums torturously against me. A slick finger follows the sensation, gently massaging around before sliding in. I gasp, instantly working to meet him.

His other hand settles on the small of my back, stilling me. "Easy, just relax for me."

I do.

I let him take over and while I can't hold back the moans and cries, I manage to let him control the pace. It's freeing, exhilarating and so *fucking* good. Two fingers work me now, curving to meet a place that I've only ever brushed against with those stupid toys from Kitt. It's not enough, and I'm tired of it.

I open my mouth, but Thatch beats me to it. Rather breathlessly, he asks, "Arlo, I need you. Are you ready?"

"Yes, Gods, yes."

Thatch's fingers and mouth slip away. The wet and warm head of his cock presses against me, but he doesn't enter yet. He leans forward, applying pressure, but it isn't enough. His lips meet the curve of my shoulder and he whispers, "There's only one God here tonight, Arlo."

And he thrusts inside me.

It's slow and smooth, giving me time to adjust, but there's something underlying the *almost* too tight way he holds my hips. The way his cock doesn't fully leave when he pulls back, and the way he hardens almost painfully inside me when he moves forward again. Like I might disappear. It takes a few thrusts and at first the red hot pressure is near unbearable, but then he's seated deep inside me and nothing has ever felt more right. That connection between us strengthens, bursting with heat and light

He breathes, body trembling and hips still.

I breathe, magick singing and heart overfull.

"Are you alright?" I ask, and he sighs. Relaxes.

Thatch murmurs, "I'm not dreaming."

And I say, "No, you're not."

Thatch moves then. It's all hips and skin and want and need and *everything*. A hand settles on my chest, pulling me flush to his front. He's shorter than I am, but the strength he holds is infinite. *He* is infinite. I've never felt safer, more loved than I do *right* now, in his arms. His other hand takes a gentle hold of my throat and I rest my head on his shoulder, eyes sliding shut as whimpers and moans pour from us both.

"Touch yourself, *leva*. Come for me."

I do, hips jerking us out of sync at the overwhelming sensation. Thatch holds me closer to him, nipping my ear. He thrusts faster, grunting against my shoulder. His beard scrapes against the flickering muscles and I gasp, stroking myself with slow and shuddering movements.

Thatch *growls* at me, clearly impatient. My face hits the mattress and he's still there at my shoulder, but teeth have replaced his beard and they're *sinking* into my skin. Ozone fills the air and the scent of something burning nearly tears me out of the moment, but then Thatch's hand knocks mine out of the way. He jacks me fiercely, fucking into me with no quarter. His teeth release my shoulder, only to latch onto my neck and catch bits of hair.

"Holy fuck, I'm—"

Coming harder than I've ever fucking come in my life. The past times we spent together were nothing compared to this, and those were so *fucking* good they fueled my fantasies for the next eleven years. Thatch doesn't stop fucking me, doesn't stop stroking my cock despite the fact I've spilled and spilled and there's nothing left. Something literally *shatters* and the air vibrates as Thatch orgasms, hand stuttering to a stop on my cock. He cries out and I can *feel* him pulsing inside me. It triggers another wave of pleasure aftershocks that elicit a soft moan from my broken chest.

Thatch's cheek comes to rest upon my shoulder, rising and falling with my heaving lungs. His heart hammers against my ribs. After a few moments, he tries to speak but has to clear his throat. He tries again, and his words are cautious. "I ... don't know what came over me. Are you alright?"

I laugh.

"Am I *alright*? I just got fucked so goddamn hard I saw stars. Yes, I'm *quite* alright, dear."

Thatch sputters, then he's laughing too.

Still Pissed

Thatch

Arlo and I sit on the roof of our cottage, passing a glass pipe back and forth between us for who knows how long. The night is considerably young, after cleaning the shattered mirror and some cuddling we decided it would be a shame to fall asleep this early. Besides, he still has a job he needs my help with, apparently.

My muscles are lax and bones warm, mind clear for the first time in days. While the herbs are wonderful, that's not what's got me feeling so good. I chance a sideways glance at Arlo, but he's already looking at me. We giggle, gaze dancing away and back again like adolescents. Smoke rolls from the distant campfire, escaping through the break in the canopy. The sounds of children playing with their new gifts have long faded, giving way to rambunctious adults whooping and hollering.

"We can go back, if you want," I say, finishing another loosely packed bowl.

Arlo shrugs, leaning back on his hands. "Nah, I'm good. Unless you want to, but I for one am peopled out."

"Peopled out. I like that one." I snort, reaching over to tuck the glass pipe inside Arlo's jacket pocket. I'm wearing his old leather one, the one he's wearing is a newer version that he insists works just fine for him.

"You ... seemed to enjoy yourself today," Arlo says, watching me with big golden eyes. His lips are sex swollen, curls tangled. There's a visible mark on his neck, barely covered by his up-turned collar. I want to feel bad about it, and I did at first, but I don't now. Arlo said he likes it, which pleases me greatly.

"I did." I kiss him gently, then brush my nose against his. Our knees knock together. My fingers curl in the hair behind his ear, then I kiss him again. He smiles against my lips, and I'm so happy it feels like I'm dreaming. I can't be. I'll die if I'm dreaming.

"You're not dreaming," Arlo Rook says, and I cry.

I cry with happiness.

With the realization that this is it, this is my life.

It's real and I get to have this, every day.

I cry, and he holds me through it all.

We lay on our backs, watching the constellations move over-head.

He tells me about a birthday party with just enough glitter and glue.

I tell him about a man who enchanted hundreds with just one string.

He tells me about waiting.

I tell him I know all about waiting.

He tells me about wayward witches seeking refuge, and how he always wondered how I knew they would find him. How I knew that would be his calling.

I tell him I didn't know, but I don't think he believes me. I'm not sure if I believe me.

He tells me about a boy who insisted he wasn't a skunk.

I tell him about lost cities.

And we kiss under the stars, lips soft and slow.

After a little while, my fingers tracing circles over his wrist, I say, "Miles."

"He asked you, didn't he?"

I glance sideways at him, he's looking at me with perhaps the most stern expression I've seen from him upon returning.

"I wondered if you knew."

Arlo nods once. "Miles came to me for help shortly after moving in." He inhales sharply. "He told me he wasn't sure if he could keep on living, not the way he was. Obviously, we didn't find anything that could help, not really. Everything was a temporary fix."

"But he's still here," I say, looking back to the stars.

"Yes, and I am so very glad that he is."

We're quiet for a time, then, "Did you do it?"

I breathe. "Yes, I did." I tell him about threads of the soul and myocardial fibers of magick. I tell him that with one singular cut, I defied the laws of the universe. Again.

Arlo stops breathing. When his chest rises again, he asks, "Is that you did? To come home?"

"Yes, and no. I bought some time, but they'll want me again. They can't force me, now, but ... I *will* be called again, some day. It will be up to me whether I answer that call. I will have a choice."

"I have a theory," Arlo says after a moment. My heart stutters. "Oh?"

"Mhm. I don't think it was Cas that broke their hold on you."

I smile, and it *hurts*. "No?"

"No. I think the day you and I made promises to each other on the beach, witnessed by an ancient stone that I'm convinced is much more than it appears, I think something broke that day, and I think something else rose in its place. I think ..." Arlo inhales deeply and I stop breathing completely. "I think you could have stayed, and I think you knew that. Maybe not at first, but when Cas made his wish, you knew. You made him promise to take care of me."

I release a breath finally, a shuddering and fracturing thing. "Are you angry with me?"

Arlo captures my hand with his, then presses his lips to my cold knuckles. Against my cracking skin he murmurs, "No. Not anymore." Arlo's eyes meet mine and they're so *golden*. "You made a promise, didn't you? To help those people."

I nod, just once. "I did, and when my assignment was complete, I was made an offer. I could go home, to you, for a short amount of time, but I would have to go back. Or, I could complete my other assignments in advance. There was, and still is really, much turmoil in the universe. I decided that I could not handle saying goodbye to you so soon, but I did not think it would take as long as it did, either."

Arlo treads very carefully, words quiet and slow. "And what happens if you don't go back, the next time you're called?"

I squeeze his hand with all my might. "We don't have to worry about that right now."

"Thatch."

"Arlo, it won't happen in your lifetime. Please."

Arlo sits up on an elbow, brows furrowed as he stares down at me. "I know why you're the last one. I want to hear you say it."

Tears sting my eyes. "That's what happened to the other Watcher, wasn't it?"

Arlo nods curtly. "They were a friend of Jamie's. I didn't know, none of us did, not at first. But then Imogen—"

A memory slashes across my eyes, stealing my vision and gouging my ear drums. I wince, groaning at the headache assaulting my temples.

"Got sick, and none of us knew why. Then Tobias touched her and he knew, he knew because he said you felt the same way——-"

Crazed screams rattle my skull and I say, "*Stop.*"

"Thatcher." Arlo pleads, and I open my eyes. He's crying, silent and fat tears stream down his cheeks. "You can't do that to me. I would wait a hundred years for you if it meant you were coming *back*. When the Watchers could choose for themselves, they all chose humanity and love and *life*. But they went mad with the calls of those who needed them, didn't they? Before dying, they went *mad*."

And then we're both sobbing under the full moons, arms tight around the other like that will stop the world from tearing us apart.

Later, after our tears have dried and we've buried tomorrow's problems, Arlo asks if I'm still up for helping him out, or if I'm tired yet.

I smile at him. "Going to tell me what this secret job is?"

He chuckles. "Don't go ruining my fun. It involves Thitwhistle's, if that helps."

"Yes." I sit up quickly, blood rushing from my head down to my toes. I blink rapidly a few times, adjusting. "Woah, that was fast."

"You're not excited or anything, are you?" Arlo asks, looking up at me with a cat's grin. His eyes are red-rimmed, and I'm sure mine are too.

"It's time," I say, perhaps more seriously than I intended to. Arlo nods, sitting up. He offers me his hand and I take it, gasping when a stone conjures to life and slides between our palms. This one is smaller, but just as smooth.

Arlo stares at me a moment, smiling quietly.

"What?"

"Nothing," He shakes his head. "I just love you."

Instantaneous smile. "I love you, too."

"Hold on," he says, then whispers, "*MochaScone,*" three times, and I laugh during all three incantations.

Arlo and I haven't talked about Thitwhistle's at all since I've returned.

I'm not quite sure why. I resided there for about a week ,over a decade ago. Yes, I poured my heart into the place during that time, wanting to leave it the best I possibly could for the person I chose as its caretaker.

I knew it was Arlo from the beginning, I think. There wasn't a place in Thitwhistle's that had gone untouched by his paintbrush, and that was one the main reasons I directed Arlo to keep it exactly the same as I had left it. While I didn't always live there,

I always visited, and the place felt more like home to me than anywhere else had, the island included.

Perhaps it's fear that's kept me from asking. Levena and its people have been affected greatly, keeping a coffee shop open could not have been high on anyone's priority list. Arlo hasn't offered news either, and I suspect he knew I wasn't quite ready yet to find out what he's done.

Which is to say, *mostly* nothing.

We arrive just inside the front door, greeting a dark room and shuttered windows. I inhale sharply, capturing books and sugar into my lungs. A little shiver goes through me when Arlo leaves my side, reaching behind us to flick on the lights. I have to blink a few times to adjust, and when I do, my hands fly to my mouth.

The hearth on the west side of the cafe sputters to life, illuminating the galaxies and constellations streaked across the ceiling and on the floor surrounding the cafe counter's raised circular dais. There are a few more round dining tables situated in the space, and only one hearth entertains upholstered furniture now instead of two.

The eastern fireplace has been replaced by a small stage, complete with microphones and speakers. On the surrounding walls are numerous instruments, all seemingly good quality but nothing over the top. There's a cork board too, filled with band schedules and other things like tutors for hire or stand-up comedy nights. The booth with painted fox prints isn't far away, but it's been elongated. Festive Yuletide decorations are scattered throughout, from wreaths to bells, silver garland to mistletoe.

"Calen's quite the musician, as you heard, and sometimes Silas plays too. Those are fun days," Arlo chuckles, hands in his pockets as we stare at the stage. "I know you said not to change anything, but ... it was needed, music. This place, it was a sanctuary for a lot of people, still is really."

I wander over to the empty and pristine pastry case, tracing a finger alongside the metal trim. "Did I ever tell you why I chose to buy Thitwhistle's?"

Arlo glances at me, betraying a hint of surprise from the other side of the counter. "No, I don't think so."

I nod, staring at a knot in the grain beside the cash register. They're the same wooden countertops, but refinished. Sanded and polished, oiled to reveal the grain's true nature. "In the more ... well, *considerably* recent years, each time I came back to Levena, I had a ritual. I took what I needed from the burrow and settled into the cottage. Then, before anything else, I came here. I would reintroduce myself to Mrs. Thitwhistle, who never treated me the same way twice, but was always kind to me no matter what."

I chuckle, barely meeting Arlo's eye when I gesture to his booth. "Then I would sit over there, with my pile of scones because Mrs. Thitwhistle always complained that I was too skinny, and a cup of coffee. I would ... people-watch."

Arlo raises a brow and I blush, but he doesn't say anything. Always patient. Always waiting.

"I don't know why, but this place ... I still have never experienced anything like it. I always thought it was Thitwhistle's doing, she had this way about her that drew in the most unique and spectacular people. I learned so much about how this world changed, and in the best of ways, from these wonderfully alive *people*. Arlo, I don't know how else to describe it."

Arlo takes my hand, squeezing softly. "It's home."

I shake my head. "No, that's not—*you* are my home, Arlo. What I'm trying to say is that I think this place has its own magick, its own ... *something*, you know? It's always been a safe and comforting place to be, but now it's something more. A sanctuary, like you said. I can feel it, there's so much good here, but ...."

I wrinkle my nose. "But there was bad here too, wasn't there?"

Arlo sighs, eyes dropping to our joined hands. "There was. But it's over now."

"You can tell me, you know. If you need to talk about it, I'm—I'm not fragile."

"I know."

"And, I know what you said, earlier." My cheeks heat with the memory, but I need to get this out. "But, if—I would understand, Arlo, if there was, well ... I would not blame you for not wanting to be alone. And if there was someone you lost that was especially dear to you, that's ... I want to be here for you."

"Oh, Thatch." Arlo squeezes my fingers impossibly tight, and then he doesn't say anything for a *long* time. When he does, his eyes flash a violent neon green. "I told you I would wait for you, and that's what I did. Yes, I was lonely, but I could never ...."

A shuddering breath overtakes him and he straightens, letting me go. "Finnegan and I were very close, I cannot deny that, especially towards the end, when it got really bad. I ... haven't told anyone else this, but ... I didn't think we would win, Thatch. I really didn't, and I was ready to give up, but Fin kept me going. He kissed me, once. I didn't kiss him back. I told him that we couldn't be that, and he respected me."

My heart pounds incredibly slowly.

I believe him with my entire heart. I ache for him. And I'm jealous of a man long dead.

"Did you love him?"

Arlo shakes his head. "No, not like that. Not like you."

I believe he *thinks* that's the truth, but my gut settles on a different answer. Arlo loved him. If there hadn't been me, or the ghost of me, I think he would've said yes. And I don't know what to do with that. Not to mention the fact I've seen how Calen, Lysander, Silas, and Felix love. How many different ways their hearts can split and merge and fill.

If Finnegan had lived, would Arlo have asked me for something similar?

Would it have ever crossed his mind?

Would I have liked Finnegan?

"Can I ...." I trail off, unsure what I'm really asking.

Arlo shoves his hands deep into his pockets. He tilts his head in a 'come hither' motion, so I follow him into one of the back rooms. He flips a switch and a singular overhead light flickers on, illuminating a storage area of sorts. Metal shelving units line the walls, cardboard boxes and plastic totes rest on the shelves. A large, run down table with some chairs haphazardly settled around it sits in the center of the room.

One shelving unit is dedicated entirely to brightly wrapped packages, and I'm drawn to them. They're neatly stacked and organized, some have curly ribbons and others have bows. Color combinations vary between blue and white, or red and green.

"I met Finnegan shortly after you left. Initially, he wanted an interview regarding my involvement with you, the Game, and the work Caspian and I had been doing. I told him no, talking to a godsdamned reporter of all things was not something I wanted to do." Arlo chuckles, eyes roving the packages. "Long story short, he convinced me."

"How?" I ask, genuinely curious.

Arlo looks at me then with a sad, but sly smile. "He said that history was meant to be remembered, not forgotten. If the one person who knew you most intimately wouldn't share your story, the *right* one, then who would? How could I say no to that?"

I flush. "You didn't—"

"Please, don't." He practically begs, startling me a little. Arlo shakes his head, rubbing his temple. "*Don't* say we didn't have to. We went through a lot, to uphold the truth. It wasn't just about you, you know. There was so much more to this."

And don't I fucking know it? I swallow, which does nothing to abate the burning sensation in my throat. "You lied to me."

He blinks, taken aback. "What?"

My hands ball into fists and I stare him dead in the eyes. Words fall out of me and there's no holding back, the anger burning in my gut is unlike anything I've felt in awhile.

"You have severely downplayed the severity of what occurred while I was gone, and I have found out through everyone else today *but* you how it affected you, and our family. I know that I'm ... too little too late, but I'm here now. I want to take care of you. I want to help you heal, because I don't think you've done that. You can keep everyone else at an arm's length and hide behind a smile, but not me."

Arlo exhales, a short and abrupt thing. "Our."

"*What?*"

He steps closer and I glare at him, arms crossing. His hands encapsulate my face anyway and I set my jaw, glowering up at him with all my might. I've brought titans to their knees, created worlds and set them aflame. I can overcome a Hedge Witch.

The thing is, I can't overcome *this* witch. *My* Hedge Witch.

"You said *our* family. Did you mean it?" Emerald magick simmers, overtaking his golden irises and dancing with his blood, illuminating his body in the most subtle of ways. The arteries and veins running up his arms and into his hands are a slight luminescent green. His palms are warm and electrified.

"Of course I did—"

He kisses me.

And I bite his lower lip, because I need him to know I'm still pissed.

But then I kiss him back.

I slide my arms around his neck. My fingers travel up his nape and into his hair, tangling in knotted waves of the deepest brown-black intermingled with silver. His hands caress down my throat, over my shoulders, and along my sides. He firmly takes a hold of my ass, pulling me closer to him. I moan into his mouth at the same moment his tongue enters mine. His cock stiffens against me and our teeth knock together in attempts for our bodies to impossibly become one.

You wouldn't know we'd sated ourselves hours before. Our desperation is palpable, the scent of magick permeates the room within seconds. I roll my hips, grinding my hard length against his. This isn't what I had planned, but I need him. I need to know he's *alive* and *here*, and that I'm *here* and *alive*.

Arlo grips my ass harder, body shaking with restrained magickal energy that is impatient, ready to meet mine once more. Arlo manages to get a few words out between my barrage of kisses. "*Ah*, Thatcher. You're driving me fucking crazy."

"Arlo, I fucking need you." I groan onto his lips, which causes his skin to tremble with a wave of vibration. I pull away ever so slightly, cupping his jaw with a firm hand. His lips are swollen and eyes dilated, chest rising and falling with heavy breaths. *I* did that to him.

"Do you need me?" I ask, because I need the words on his mischievous tongue.

"More than anything," He whispers, brushing his nose against mine. I lean forward, beard scratching against his. Goosebumps rise along my arms at the sensation, and I relish it.

I kiss his throat, sliding the hand once in his hair down his chest, over stomach muscles which flutter upon meeting me. "Thatch, let me taste you. Please."

I cup his erection and he moans. The vibrations skim over my lips and I can't help but chuckle. "Once upon a time you teased me for my manners, and now look at you. Asking so nicely."

"I don't recall you being so shameless." Arlo manages, breathing heavily.

"Life is too short to not have some fun, *leva*. You've taught me that. You want to taste me? Then hit your knees."

He does. I nearly come from the sight of him dropping to the ground so eagerly, fingers fumbling over my button. I rest my hand on the back of his head, fingers sliding through his waves. Cool air meets my aching cock and I sigh when Arlo takes me in hand. He looks up at me, long lashes shuttering over his eyes.

I bend down and press a kiss to the top of his head, leaving truth there. "You're so beautiful, Arlo."

Arlo smiles at me like I'm heaven and earth, then slides my cock past those upturned lips. I groan, fingers flexing in his hair. "Put your tongue out," I murmur, and he obeys. I thrust into his mouth, hips rolling long and slow. His eyes flutter shut, throat working as I go deeper and deeper. He swallows, nose pressed to ginger curls, and I shudder at the sensation.

"Fuck, so good for me." I mutter, and Arlo *groans* at the sentiment. I caress his cheek and his watering eyes open, unfocused as they settle on me. "You like that?"

He nods the littlest bit and whines, hands settling on my hips as his chest presses against my thigh. I don't miss the sensation of his thumb swiping across my illuminated soulmark, and I love him so much for it. Gently, he rocks me forward and back again. The flick of a tongue swipes along the underside of my cock and air hitches in my chest. I bring my other hand up, holding his face firmly with both hands now. His own soulmark brightens when I do, and his pupils dilate until there is only a sliver of golden-green.

"You'll be good and tell me if it's too much, right?"

Arlo hums, and I withdraw my cock from his mouth. He whines again, but I shush him with a thumb to his spit slicked lips. "Tell me, Arlo."

He kisses my thumb ever so gently. "I'll be good. Please, don't stop. I'll be good."

"I know you will." I nod once, then slide my cock back inside his hot mouth. He moans like I've given him the best thing, fingers digging into my sides. I hold his gorgeous face in my hands, and fuck him.

I thrust into his throat with deep, unrelenting thrusts. Drool wets the hairs at the base of my cock and teeth scrape against my shaft every now and then, but I can't stop. I pump into him, chasing away my frustrations and everything I cannot change. Pants and grunts escape me, and that little thought crosses the back of my mind again.

You're ruining him, you're being too rough, you have to stop.

But my stars, every time I slow down or loosen my hold on his face, Arlo nearly weeps with the loss. His eyes open just the slightest bit and he stares up at me like I'm *something*. Tears spill from his eyes and the sight of him being absolutely *wrecked* awakens something primordial and feral inside of me. My balls tighten and magick, his and mine both, rides down my spine.

"Arlo, come with me. Get your fingers on your cock and come with me, right *now*."

He obeys. His eyes blissfully close when his hand dives under the waistband of his pants. He keens around my cock, a broken and needy sound. I watch his movements begin, then stutter to a stop, then try again.

"*Arlo*," I grit out, and the lights pop. He groans harshly around me, jerking himself furiously at the sound of my voice. I manage his name one more time, then thrust forward harshly and bury myself in his throat. I release, and release, and *release*. I cradle his head in my hands, holding him in place. His throat works against my bare thigh, swallowing everything I have to offer.

Then, ever so gently, I withdraw from his mouth. His temple rests on my thigh, hands sliding from my hips, down to wrap around my leg. I pet his hair, staring down at this gorgeous man that has only ever needed someone to take care of him.

He looks up at me after a moment with a shy smile. He's absolutely debauched, still entirely dressed but wearing the look of someone who's been properly fucked. And because he's Arlo, he says, "For someone who says they're not a God, you fuck like one all the same."

I laugh and laugh. "My ego cannot handle any more of this God nonsense. Come now, let's get you fixed up."

"You're the one who said earlier—-"

"I know I know, don't remind me. I was feeling quite full of myself." I grumble, helping Arlo to his feet.

He kisses me, long and sweet. "That was awesome."

I smile, but there's a wobble to it. "You didn't ... it wasn't too much?"

"Thatch," Arlo says, kissing between my brows. "If it makes you nervous, you don't have to ... be that way."

I give him a look. "That's not what I asked."

He chuckles. "Thatch, I am one hundred percent enjoying whatever *this* is. And I'm also up for other things, if you don't want to hold the reins, or if it's nerve wracking for you. I'll understand. But please, trust me when I say, I'll tell you if something is too much. Just like I know you would tell me, right?"

I nod. "Right. I'm not … I don't know why, but seeing you like that, it, it—I like it." My voice trails off and a flush overtakes my throat. Arlo *laughs*, mussing my hair.

"You are a complex man, and I love every intricacy you have. Always."

And how could I not kiss him?

Again, and again, and again.

This Is How

Arlo

I corral my dishevelment the best I can, cleaning up in the washroom before reconvening with Thatch in the storage room once more. He's staring at the packages, arms crossed and brow furrowed. When he sees me coming, that crease between his brows smooths out and he *smiles*. That furious light hasn't left his eyes and we've uncovered so *much* today, but he smiles at me when I enter the room like we haven't spent all day together.

"Hey, handsome," I say, smoothing my hands down the front of his unbuttoned waistcoat.

He chuckles, knocking my forehead with his. "Hello again. So, tell me. What are these for?"

I grin. "Is the suspense killing you?"

Thatch stares at me, deadpan. "Not being in our bed is killing me. I'm too old for these late night romps with you."

I laugh. "I'll remember that, *old* man."

Thatch's lips twitch, a small and oh so wonderful thing. I remove a neatly organized package from the shelf, passing it to Thatch. "You can open it, we'll rewrap it after."

He raises a brow. "Sure?" I nod, and the moment I do he's ripping and tearing into the package. I laugh again, and he looks up from the package almost sheepishly. "It's fun, shut it."

I put my hands up. "I didn't say a word, love."

The blue and white paper falls to the ground, taking with it a curled milky white ribbon which bounces when it hits the floor. Books and a thin wooden box with a puzzle inside of it rest in Thatch's hands, this particular set is a children's pack. The bindings are clearly worn, some more than others. He reverently traces a finger over the title of a book full of fairy tales, lips parted.

"Certain books have sun damaged pages or other small flaws, but I wouldn't classify any of these as no good, just well loved. There are a select few that are brand new, those are the ones that have been donated by those in the know during the year. It's kind of a secret, by the way." I pick up the ribbon from the floor, curling its length around my finger. I breathe.

"It was Fin's before it was mine, this endeavor. Before we met, Fin would put together these packages for the kids growing up in the poorer districts. If they *did* have families, they were incredibly poor for one reason or another. Kids who fell through the school's cracks, kids who Dusan or I could not help, or really did not know how to, at the time. Then we met, and he let me in on the secret. Everything he had to give, he either bought himself or scoured the libraries and bookstores when they would give them away. Of course, having a witch helped move things along immensely, as far as trying to move as many packages as we could in one night. We did it for three years, and then ...."

Silence chokes me, and I *breathe* with every ounce of willpower I have.

Thatch stares up at me, eyes watery but firm and kind. "I would like to have met him, Arlo. I truly mean it. He sounds like an incredible man, and I'm so glad you continued this for him. I think he would be oh so proud of you. I know that I am."

How many times can a man cry in the span of twenty-four hours?

Apparently, I'm still finding out.

With great care, Thatch places the books back on the shelf. He embraces me, grounding me while I weep for what was and never will be. He whispers, "It's okay."

And, "You are so dear to me, and I love you. I love you. I love you."

And, "Come now, Arlo. They're counting on us."

He kisses me, hands on my wet cheeks. I kiss him back, because I can, because he's here. Because I love him. Because he's mine.

"Okay, let's do this. I'm good, I'm okay."

Thatcher Gaillot smiles at me. "I know."

He blushes then, eyes darting to the books. "How exactly do you plan on doing this? Who do they go to? There's so many."

I wipe my eyes with the back of my hand, laughing a little. "Lots of reconnaissance, I assure you. Mostly keeping in touch with foster families and the Nightingale, they're the—"

"The fiercest mobster in all the North," Thatch says, grinning knowingly. "I still haven't heard the story of how you managed to make friends with them."

I give him a tight smile. "Fin, they were friends. Well, more like family, but that's how I met them. The Nightingale was an incredible ally to have, and we still keep in touch. They've been wanting to meet you."

Thatch's cheeks flush. "Oh, I'd like that. I'd like that very much."

"Me too."

We stare at each other for a moment, like imbeciles.

Thatch clears his throat, glancing at the shelf.

"Did you have something in mind?"

He fidgets with the hems of his long sleeves. "Well, if you'd like, I could send these on their way pretty easily. I don't want to impose, though."

"That'd be fine. I normally have Felix help me, I glamor the gifts and he moves them. There's not many people on the streets at midnight, but if there are, we can avoid them easily enough."

Thatch chuckles, looking up at me with a devilish gleam in his eye. It heats me up from the inside out. "All we have to do is open the front door, and you'll have to touch me, show me where they're going. I'll take care of the rest."

You'll have to touch me.

"I can do that," I say, bending down until my lips meet his curls. I picture each and every person in Levena who needs something extra this Yuletide, because not all of the packages are intended for children, just most of them. There are a few for parents, and more still for loners who can barely afford the basics. I inhale before pulling away, heart settling. "I love you, Thatch."

"And I you." He beams up at me, then stands on his tiptoes and kisses my nose. "Go on."

I do as he says, our shoes thud on the old floors as he follows me out. This would normally take hours and an incredible amount of magick, and my bones are so damn tired. Perhaps Thatch isn't the only old one around here. I open the front door, bell tinkling as I laugh a little at the thought. We step into the crisp night, boots crunching in the snow.

Thatch cocks his head at me. "What?"

I shrug. "Nothing, just happy, I suppose."

"Me too Arlo, me too." He takes my hand, squeezing once before letting go. Thatch stands tall, hands on his hips. "Ready?"

"As I'll ever be," I say, even though I really have no idea what to expect from Thatcher Gaillot. And that's just the way I like it.

He brings his palms together over his heart. Closes his eyes. Breathes.

The night air *hums*.

I swear to the *Gods* the ground shakes beneath my feet, a small tremor that throws me off balance momentarily. Thatch is an unmoving pillar, lips wordlessly moving as the night *cracks* to life. Thick, dark clouds roll in from the east, blanketing the moons at the same time street lights wink out one by one. A blinding, pale blue light emanates from Thatch's chest, right where the heart of this world beats, and beats, and *beats*.

Thatcher Gaillot opens his eyes, flashing sapphire irises that bore into my very spirit, flaying me open like never before. It's then I realize this isn't about presents, not really. He's revealing himself to me, his true primordial and ancient form that transcends earthly origins. He is doing what he never could before, and I'm bearing witness to something unheard of.

I fall to my knees, magick coursing through me violently. It says *submit*, and *acknowledge*, and *God*, he is *your* God.

Tiny, swirling vortexes of endless light replace freckles.

Eternal flames cascade down his shoulders in vicious curls and tendrils.

The little mole under his eye is now a galaxy, and his scars play host to shooting stars.

He *smiles* at me, and it's creation itself. Tears spill onto the snow and my hands *shake*, the veins up and down my hands and wrists are a burning green.

He says, "Hello," and "Hi," and, "It's still me, don't be afraid. Please, don't be afraid."

I breathe, just barely.

He hums that simple old holiday tune from earlier. I'm quite certain now he has an attachment to it. Power ricochets in the confines of our little world, splitting the tension in the air with an audible *crack* that could fool some into thinking it was thunder. Then something *whistles* out of the store, too fast to track. Again, and again.

Thatch offers me his hand, humming his song. I'm afraid to touch him, to ruin him, but I know he's expecting that. I slide my mortal hand into his. I gasp when my energy connects with his, my frenzied magick swiftly relaxes to such a degree it's near orgasmic. He smiles and helps me up, paying no mind to the invisible packages whizzing out of the shop to who knows where.

He asks, "Are you afraid?"

"No. Not ever, not of you."

He kisses me then, slowly and softly, like we have all the time in the world.

"Arlo, Arlo. *Arlo.*"

I blink, eyelids reluctantly parting. Blue, sky blue. Red, shining copper.

"Thatcher? Did you have a bad dream?"

He's smiling wide, voice quavering. "No, no bad dreams. It's morning, we slept right through."

"Oh. Why—"

"It's *Yuletide*, Arlo. It's *snowing*, and it's Yuletide. Can we get up, *please*?"

I laugh, wrapping my arms around him. He's naked and I am too. I don't quite remember getting to bed, but I have the vague memory of being carried like a child, my head on Thatch's shoulder. Thatch squeals, peppering the junction of my neck and shoulder with kisses and love bites. "*Arlo*," He begs, stretching my name out.

"Alright, alright. Find us some clothes, then I'll get up," I say, kissing Thatch's forehead. He scrambles out of bed like a rocket and I laugh. "What are you so excited for?"

"I don't know!" He yells from the closet. "There's such ... I don't know! There's something in the air, can't you feel it? Doesn't your magick just *sing*? I want hot chocolate, and to sit by the fire in the den while you tell me stories. I want Calen and Felix and Silas and Lysander to come over, and even the damned goat. I want it all!"

I close my eyes and smile.

A few minutes later his hand encircles my ankle, literally *pulling* me out of bed. I land on my ass with an undignified grunt, taking Thatch down with me. My hands take a firm hold of his face and I kiss him, pulling him down into my lap. He straddles me, his cold and naked body fits against mine so perfectly. The bed frame digs into my back but I don't care.

He says, "Arlo, Arlo. *Arlo*."

And I say, "I want to make love to you, Thatch. Let me love you."

He whimpers, "Please," and "Yes," and "*Arlo*."

Thatch

His tongue says good morning to mine and I take a hold of our cocks without preamble, stroking us with both hands. He groans into my mouth, pulling back long enough to messily wet two fingers. We meet again in a collision of lips and teeth, his slick fingertips encircle my hole before entering, just one at first. I gasp, stealing his breath.

"Oh yes, please." I moan, hands stuttering and hips desperately working for more.

"I don't want to hurt you, be patient." Arlo murmurs into my beard, and I *sigh*.

I calm my fervent energy the best I can, breathing against his neck as I stroke us again, slower and with intent this time. It doesn't take long for heat and pleasure to overwhelm me, and I just *need* him. He works another finger inside me, kissing down my jaw and throat as he stretches me. I shudder, the nails of my free hand digging into his shoulder.

"Arlo, please. *Please.*"

"I'm right here, right here. Do you want—"

But I already know what he's going to say, and I spit in my hand. His eyes *widen* when I slick his cock with the moisture, then sit up and position him properly. He says, "Thatch," and that's all because I sink down on his cock. It's so unbearably tight and there's a red-hot sensation, then he's past that tight ring and we both cry out.

"Oh fuck," I moan, hands gripping his shoulders as I ride his cock, working him further and further into me. His hands are firmly set on my hips, a thumb over my soulmark. Always.

"Fuck is right, oh my Gods, Thatch. Oh my—"

We settle flush to the other then, and I rock my hips. His eyes shut, irises rolling when he thrusts up into me. There's so *much* of him and I'm so fucking full, but the energy within in me screams for more. I need to feel him for days, or it will never be enough. I grip the hair at the back of his neck and his eyes fly open.

I say, "Fuck me, Arlo. I need you to fuck me. Can you do that?"

And the witch growls, "*Yes.*"

He sits up, feet flat on the floor, and I gasp at the change in position. His fingers dig into my soft sides, gripping with everything he's got.

And he thrusts up into me with such goddamn reckless abandon that I'm quite sure the house is *shaking* with it. There's no matching it, no moving with him. I hold on for dear life, fingers tangled in his hair and teeth sinking into his shoulder. I cry out with nothing but pleasure, my cock flushed and leaking between us, achingly hard.

The sounds of slick skin slapping against skin fills the room, along with Arlo's grunts and snarls. His eyes are no longer gold, but a fierce green that screams magick. He says, "You're so fucking *tight*, do you know how long I've waited to fuck you, Thatcher?"

Before I can answer, he *flips* us. I'm on my back, knees hooked over his shoulders and pressed to my chest. His cock presses against my prostate and I shudder, there's something different about this angle and sensation. One of his big hands takes a hold of my chin, gripping tight while the other rests by my head. My cock jerks, slapping against my stomach.

Arlo thrusts once, a long and powerful thing that alights my spine instantly. His hand on my face squeezes. "*Answer* me."

"Too fucking long."

"That's right."

And I'll be honest.

I had thought it couldn't get better between us.

But right then, Arlo proves to me a fact that I've only wondered at.

Things will *only* get better. Each time will always be *more* than the last.

Arlo's hips work and his eyes *shine*. His balls slap against my ass, his cock slides in and out of me with such force that my own jerks with precum on each of his long thrusts. His hand leaves my chin and gently cups my jaw. His forehead presses to mine and he kisses me with such a tenderness that contrasts his violent thrusting, and *yes*.

"*Yes*," I moan, tangling my fingers in his hair.

He whispers into my mouth, "Stroke yourself, come with me. I'm going to come, *come* with me."

And I do. He doesn't slow down, but he doesn't have to. I tug three solid times, then spill between us with an intensity that has me crying out his name. When the heat splashes across his chest, Arlo's hips stutter and he groans, cock stiffening impossibly further deep, *deep* inside me. He kisses me through it, holding my face all the while.

His arms and my legs shake, and for a moment we just stare at the other, grinning dopily. I'm the first to laugh.

He does too, asking, "What?" through his giggle fit.

I say, "Happy Yuletide, *leva*."

Arlo Rook *smiles* at me. "Happy Yuletide, my love"

He withdraws, kissing me through the loss. My arms encircle his neck, legs around his waist, and he stands with me in his arms. Like he did so long ago, Arlo carries me to the tub. This time, when he fills the tub with soap and water, we laugh and splash each other, wondering aloud how Felix and the other's night went. I don't remind him of the first time we met, and he doesn't promise that he won't forget me. We don't have to, and I've never felt more alive.

Felix

"Are you sure this is a good idea?"

"You worry too much honey, it'll be fine."

"It's *darling*, not honey. Get it right." Silas grumbles, knocking my shoulders with his. I nearly drop the platter in my hands, but thankfully Lysander rights it before I do. The pendant hanging from the collar around his neck shines in the clear mid-morning sun, and when he catches me looking at it, my soulmate blushes furiously.

"He's right, you *do* worry too much," Calen says through a mouthful of cheese, popping bits into their mouth as we approach Dad's Cottage.

"Someone's got to." Silas remarks, but there's a lightness to it.

"Do you think they're up yet?" Calen asks, feeding Tino a cheese cube. The ferret chitters from their chest pocket, eating happily. "They weren't back when we went to bed, and who knows what else kept them up so late."

"Better be," I say, fingers tapping the underside of the platter filled with breakfast appropriate leftovers from yesterday. "Besides, you really think Pesto would let them sleep in?"

"Definitely not," Silas says, then hums long and low upon hearing what I do.

We're at the front door. Silas stands beside me and my other companions are behind me. Lysander rests a hand on my shoulder, squeezing once in a fashion that is so like Dad that I can't help but smile up at him. There's music playing inside, loud and full of strings. The curtains are pulled back from the windows, and if I look hard enough I can just make out the silhouette of two people dancing. A short scream from the goat himself breaks through the music, then is followed by laughter. So *much* of it.

I blow out harsh, frigid air in a heavy burst from between my lips.

"You alright Felix?" Calen asks, a hand cupping my elbow that's squished against Silas' side. In one fashion or another, my people touch me. Center me.

I nod, huffing out a quiet laugh. "Yeah, it just ... it sounds happy in there, you know? How long has it been since we've come over and it hasn't been *quiet*?"

Silas kisses my cheek in a rare show of public affection, and I blush instantaneously despite the years shared between us. He doesn't always care for sexual intimacy, and kisses oftentimes feel that way to him, but not always. Hands, that is how he shows his love. A hand in mine. On the back of my neck. *Other* places, if he's feeling it.

I sigh, giving him a shy smile. "Thanks, darling."

"We love you," Silas says, and Calen nods furiously with tears in their eyes.

Lysander kisses the top of my head, murmuring, "So much."

"Are you four going to come in, or stand there like sweet idiots?" Arlo asks, standing in the open doorway with an arm slung around Thatch's shoulders. Both of their hair is wet and curling, and they're dressed in pajamas with hot chocolate staining the corners of their lips.

Calen bursts from between Silas and I, sweeping the platter out from my hands as they practically dance their way inside, leaving a kiss on Arlo and Thatch's cheeks before disappearing. Thatch's fingers cover the place where Calen's lips pressed, and he laughs a little. He says, "Well, come in, come in. Tell me Silas, what did you get for Yuletide?"

"New guitar strings. Jamie is very practical," Silas says, ducking his head as he walks past them. Lysander is next, flushing intensely when Thatch asks him the same question. Arlo, to his credit, does not laugh. He stares at me, a quiet smile on his face.

Lysander says, "It was very nice. He did good. Here, this is for you." He shoves a box towards Thatch, one I helped him package late last night. I found a cloak to go with the cloak pin, and the ring is accompanied by a larger twin that Serena crafted with her illusion work, turning a simple band into something more.

"Oh, that's—well, thank you," Thatch says, scratching at his beard in confusion, watching Lysander disappear with all the agility of a rabbit. Thatch looks to me then, still standing on their doorstep with my hands empty. Thatch opens his arms to me, lips twitching nervously. "Felix, oh Felix. You did so well yesterday."

I hug him. I hunch over, face burying into his neck, and breathe. There's flashes leaking from his skin into mine, and there's nothing I can do to stop them. I almost wonder if it's intentional. A glimpse of Calen, Silas, and I baking with him yesterday, or attempting to. A twinkle in Arlo's eye, his head going back as he *laughs*. Lysander's face illuminated by the fire, his hand held by someone who knows what it's like to be lonely. Calen, playing and dancing well into the night.

And I think, this is how we heal.

The Radickal Magickal Gazette

December 21st

Residents of Levena woke up to a surprise for the ages this Yuletide morning. An unprecedented snow squall buried the city streets last night and was enough to impede all traffic, keeping families close together for the holidays. If you do happen to step outside, you'll be faced with endless sled tracks winding down the roads, rosy cheeked children trekking up and down the streets as they race each other. You might be struck with a snowball packed with the oddest snow, flakes of silver and gold intermingled with naturally occurring ice, and magick. The sunny atmosphere is full of it, magick and goodwill. While the snow stopped falling at dawn, no one is in a hurry to go anywhere today.

There is also rumor spreading between those who play under the winter sun, they bring the gossip back to their families like the well wrapped presents many claim magickally appeared beneath their evergreen decorated hearths during the night. As of lunchtime, every household that I spoke to confessed to receiving a horde of personalized and much needed gifts. For some it was books and puzzles, for others it was new boots that didn't soak through or a jacket to replace the one they'd been hanging onto for years but didn't do much in the way of keeping them warm anymore. The variety spreads from cooking mixes in glass jars to watercolor sets, small guitars that match larger ones for a parent and child to learn on, together. One particular person, an older mother with older children visiting for the holiday, was gifted a pair of knitting needles and skeins upon skeins of yarn, a craft she had forgotten in her youth but she might just pick back up again now, because why not?

The most whispered of gossip dares to suggest the impossible.

Was this the work of a Phantom?

Merry Yuletide to all, and don't forget to hold your loved ones close.

-O.M

About the Author

A fantasy punk author with young witch vibes, endless coffee stains, and a craving for adventure.

Aelina's work is heavily influenced by their love of the outdoors and a need for inclusive fiction.

Visit https://aelinaisaacs.com for information on their other books, playlists and more.

Join the Crew of Misfits for free novellas, book updates and steamy art pieces.

@neshamapublishing on Instagram and TikTok, @noahhawthorneauthor on Tumblr